DANNY ORLIS
AND THE
BEWILDERED RUNAWAY

DANNY ORLIS

AND THE

BEWILDERED RUNAWAY

BERNARD PALMER

Danny Orlis and the Bewildered Runaway
© 2023 by Bernard Palmer
All rights reserved. First edition 1971.
Second edition 2024.

Scripture quotations from The Authorized (King James) Version. Rights in the Authorized Version in the United Kingdom are vested in the Crown. Reproduced by permission of the Crown's patentee, Cambridge University Press.

Cover image: Adobe Firefly
Character illustrations: John Ball
Editor: Charlene Miskimen

Aneko Press *Youth*
www.anekopress.com
Aneko Press, Life Sentence Publishing, and our logos are trademarks of Life Sentence Publishing, Inc.
203 E. Birch Street
P.O. Box 652
Abbotsford, WI 54405

JUVENILE FICTION / Religious / Christian / Action & Adventure
Paperback ISBN: 979-8-88936-068-1
eBook ISBN: 979-8-88936-069-8
10 9 8 7 6 5 4 3 2 1
Available where books are sold

CONTENTS

CHAPTER 1

JUST LIKE OLD TIMES - ALMOST

Sandy Cole moved to the picture window that overlooked their wide expanse of snow-covered yard and watched the cars inching along the icy street. Her dad and mom would be home in a few minutes, and she looked forward to that.

It hadn't been so long ago that she dreaded being with both of them at the same time, but things had been different and more enjoyable at home lately. Her dad practically never went out at night anymore. He stayed home to watch television with them or spent the evening reading or visiting with friends. He even helped her with her math homework.

Mrs. Cole didn't seem to be running frantically from one activity to another either. She didn't attend nearly as many committee meetings and luncheons as she had a few weeks ago. She even began to give excuses rather than play bridge so often, and that was something different for her. Everybody said that she would rather play bridge than eat. In the last month Sandy's parents were at the country club so seldom, some of the members began to wonder if the Coles were dropping out.

She was so excited about the change that had come into her home that she talked often with DeeDee Davis who, with her brothers Del and Doug, lived at the Danny Orlis home.

"Dad says that he's going to drop out of the country club if he finds that it's a temptation for him to start drinking again," she said with pride in her voice. "He says that he's not drinking now, and he's not going to let anything influence him to start in again."

"That's good." DeeDee had never been around anyone who drank, so she didn't actually know what it was like to be in Sandy's position, but her friend confided everything to her. She knew about the torture Sandy had been in when her dad was coming home drunk.

"I'm so proud of him now. I feel like shouting to everybody that my dad doesn't drink anymore."

Sandy went on to tell DeeDee how much happier they all were now that her dad didn't get drunk. She told and retold about the good times they were having as a family. DeeDee really hadn't appreciated the nights when Danny and Kay played Scrabble with her and her brothers or they popped popcorn or had a rousing family Ping-Pong tournament. Yet, as Sandy called her attention to it, she became increasingly aware of the fact that she and the boys should be thankful for the exciting, happy home life that was theirs.

"And there's something else I've got to tell you, DeeDee," Sandy said, her voice a thin whisper, "if you'll promise not to tell anyone."

"I won't tell anyone."

"Dad says he's going to buy mom a new designer coat this year, and I think she'll have her old one restyled for me. It will be just perfect."

DeeDee gasped. She couldn't help it. "A designer coat of your own?" She didn't dream anything like that ever happened.

"We were looking at it last night. The material in Mom's old coat is so nice we don't think anyone will know that mine isn't brand-new." She drew herself up proudly. "I'll probably be the only girl in Fairview with a designer coat."

In spite of herself, DeeDee Davis felt jealous. She tried to think of something nice to say about the coat her friend would be getting, but while she was still struggling with the words, Sandy went on.

"And we're going to remodel my room again. Dad said that Mom could redecorate the living room, too, and get some new dining room furniture if she wants."

"I think your house looks nice the way it is."

"It's all right." Sandy shrugged indifferently. "But

we get tired of the same old thing after a while. We like to get new things."

DeeDee changed the subject so she wouldn't have so much trouble in not showing how she felt. After all, Sandy had so much, and she didn't have anything. It wasn't fair at all.

*   *   *

Del Davis had been wanting to go out to Barney Aubichon's cabin and see the old Indian trapper for the last two Saturdays, but first, he had too much homework, and the next week his Sunday school class went ice skating. On this particular Saturday, however, he was determined to do it. He saddled his horse and rode out to the old Indian's little log cabin. Barney had seen him through the trees and was waiting for him in the doorway, as usual.

"I want you to come in the house," Barney said, buttoning his parka and limping out into the snow. "But I've got something to show you first."

He took Del across the clearing to an old shed.

"What is it?" Del asked excitedly.

Instead of answering, Barney lifted the lid on a small box just inside the door.

"A rabbit! Where'd you get him?"

"I found him in my bird snare a few days ago. His leg was hurt so bad I was afraid I was going to have to kill him, but I decided to see if I could patch his leg up and keep him alive until you came around."

Del reached out tenderly and touched the little rabbit on the top of his head. The tiny animal had long since gotten over his fear of man. He pressed his head against the boy's fingers as though he enjoyed the gentle caress.

"He's a cute little guy, isn't he?"

Barney's grin spread across his broad face. "I fixed a little box for you to carry him in."

Del hadn't expected there would be any visitors at the Orlis home when he went inside to show the rabbit to Kay and DeeDee, but Sandy Cole was there. His first impulse was to turn and leave as quickly as possible, but while he was deciding what to do, she spied him. There was no chance to retreat.

"Hello, Del!" Her eyes fluttered as she spoke his name.

Frantically he glanced about, but there was no way he could leave without being rude. He had to stay and face her.

"Hello." He spoke reluctantly, as though it hurt even to talk to her.

"It's so good to see you, Del," she said softly, smiling. "What have you got?"

"Oh, nothing." Involuntarily he took a step backward. "At least it isn't very much. It's just something Barney gave me. I thought I'd bring it in and show it to Kay and DeeDee."

"Can I see, too?" She embarrassed him with her childishness.

She blinked at him flirtatiously, and he felt like asking her if she had something in her eye. Then he decided to try to ignore her. He opened the box Barney had prepared for the rabbit. DeeDee and Kay came over to look, too, but they were a couple of steps behind Sandy. She stared down at the little rabbit, squealing with delight.

"Oh, it's a Peter Rabbit! How cute!" Her big eyes fastened admiringly on Del as though he had done something very wonderful in bringing the rabbit home. "Where did you get him?"

He told them how Barney had found the rabbit and brought him back to his cabin. "And he took care of him until I went out there this morning. He gave him to me to take care of."

"I think he's the cutest thing!" Sandy looked up at Del, her eyes shining. "Do you think it would be all right if I held him for one little old minute?"

"I suppose so," he grumbled uneasily. He didn't know why it was that Sandy affected him the way she did. Whenever she came around, he felt as though he wanted to run and hide. "But be real careful. His leg's still awfully sore."

"I'll be extra careful with him." Tenderly she took the little rabbit in her hands, stroking his head, and talking baby talk to him.

"A lot of people like animals, but I think it's adorable the way you get the animals to like *you*."

DeeDee looked up at her brother and snickered. She didn't want to, but she couldn't help it. He looked so miserable and helpless.

"You know, that little bunny rabbit looks up at you with such trust in his eyes. He just knows that you're going to take care of him."

DeeDee snickered again. Del glared at his sister.

"And I've been fascinated by Blackie, too." She took a step or two forward and looked up at him, still blinking. "Do you suppose I could get your pet crow to talk to me sometime?"

"I don't know." Del felt the color creeping up in his cheeks. "You'll just have to try. You can never tell what Blackie's going to do."

Her eyes widened. "Oh, Del! Would you *really* take me out and show me Blackie? *Would* you?"

Del Davis grumbled under his breath as he put on his parka and went out into the cold winter air with Sandy Cole. He'd know better than to get involved with a girl like her again, that was for sure. He knew better than to get involved with *any* girl. All they could do was cause a guy problems. The only thing he was glad about was that Doug wasn't around, but he supposed DeeDee would tell him about it as soon as he came in.

* * *

Sandy was glad she had gone out to visit DeeDee that day. She hadn't noticed before how cute Del was. She didn't think she liked him quite as well as she liked Doug, but then Doug was on the basketball team, and all the girls were crazy about him. Del was different.

She was thinking that she would have to manage to get out to the Orlis home the next Saturday as Danny pulled into the Cole's drive and let her out. Her dad's car was parked in the driveway.

Fear made her heart race. It was strange that he was home at this time of the day, even on Saturday. He should be downtown! Unless – she suddenly felt a chill – unless he had gone back on his word and had started to drink again.

Things had gone so smoothly at home that she had almost forgotten that something like this could happen. Now all her doubts and fears came rushing back. She hurried up the steps and into the house.

Sandy burst into the living room so suddenly that she startled her parents. They both jerked around quickly to stare at her.

"Sandy!" Mom's voice was thin and excited. "What is it? What's wrong?"

For an instant the girl could not move or speak. Her anxious stare read the scene in the living room. Mom and Dad were sitting across from each other, faces gray and drawn. There was something wrong. Something terribly wrong. She could tell at a glance.

"Daddy!"

He eyed her sadly and then looked away.

"What is it, Daddy?" She moved toward him, as though in a dream. "What's happened?"

Mrs. Cole spoke harshly. "She asked you! Go ahead! Answer her!"

At first Sandy supposed her dad had been drinking again, but she soon saw that was not the case. His eyes were clear, and his face didn't have that flushed, puffy look she had come to associate with his drinking bouts.

"I–" He tried but could not bring himself to say it.

"What is it?" Desperation edged Sandy's voice.

"He's the one who caused the mess." Her voice grated irritably. "He's the one who ought to tell you."

At last Mr. Cole raised his head. "I–I've been wanting to tell both of you about this for the last several weeks, but I–I kept thinking I could work things out. I can't keep it from you any longer. The bank won't loan me any more money, and–"

His wife broke in belligerently. "What he's trying to say is that he's neglected that business of his until he's gone bankrupt!"

Sandy's eyes widened. She knew that being bankrupt meant her father had lost his money, but she couldn't understand that. Her parents had always had plenty of money, more than almost anyone else in town. She only had the vaguest idea of what her mother was saying.

Mr. Cole leaned forward intently. "It's really not

as bad as it sounds. I've still got my health, and I know a lot about merchandising. I can salvage a little money and go somewhere else. I can get a good job until things work out so we can get another start." He turned to his wife, desperation darkening his eyes. "We can manage."

Sandy couldn't see what there was to be so disturbed about. She had always trusted her dad. And he had always had money when they wanted anything. If he said they could manage, there was no doubt in her mind that they could. But she didn't even think her mother had heard him. She spoke woodenly, like some sort of expressionless machine.

"I always felt that we had some measure of security, Sandy and I. I thought there would always be some way that we could get along, regardless of whether you were able to stay sober or not, but now–" She gestured widely. "Now we don't have anything! I'll never be able to face my friends again!"

The silence hung like an icy cloud between them.

"You've never been in want, dear."

"Don't you 'dear' me!" she exploded. "You've ruined the past few years with your drinking, and now you're ruining the future!"

He reached out toward her, but she jerked away.

"I can take care of you. I've got contacts in Minneapolis where I can have a good job next week. And in a year or two I'll have my own business again, and we'll be able to live better than we've ever lived. I'm not finished yet."

Her glance discouraged him, and he stopped helplessly.

"More of your wild promises! You kept telling us that now that you've quit drinking, everything was going to be all right. We were going to be able to live as well as ever and be happier than we'd ever been. But what's happened? We're broke! Bankrupt!" Her voice raised. "When you were doing all that drinking, I tried to warn you. I told you what was going to happen if you didn't straighten up and start taking care of your business."

"But I *did* quit drinking!" His desperation was giving way to anger, and he shouted too.

"After it's too late!" She burst into tears. "I don't know how we're going to manage now, Sandy! We'll probably lose the house and–and everything!"

Mr. Cole studied his daughter's face helplessly. "I–I'm sorry, Sandy," he said softly.

His wife broke in again. "You're sorry! A lot of good that's going to do now! This is all your fault! And your being sorry for the rest of your life isn't going to change anything!"

Something within Mr. Cole exploded. "All you've ever done is nag, nag, nag! I'm sick and tired of it!"

He jumped to his feet.

"Daddy!"

"Now you're trying to turn Sandy against me!"

Instantly her parents were shouting at each other once more, as bitterly as she had ever heard them arguing. At last Mr. Cole grabbed his coat. "Goodbye!"

Sandy took a few steps in his direction, as though to follow him. "Where are you going, Daddy?"

"I'm going someplace where I don't have to listen to that mother of yours!" He stormed out, slamming the door behind him.

Mrs. Cole cried silently for a moment or two after he was gone. "I knew it wouldn't last! Now he's gone out to get drunk again! If he hasn't done enough to us already, he's got to start drinking!"

Sandy thought her mom could have been more understanding in view of the progress Mr. Cole had made with his drinking problem. But then, she realized regretfully, being understanding had never been one of her mother's strong points.

CHAPTER 2

SOMEBODY, DO SOMETHING!

Sandy Cole was not listening to her mother's bitter tirade. The words bounced against unhearing ears. She was thinking about her dad. She knew that look on his face, the hurt and anger in his eyes. She tried to make herself believe that she was mistaken, but deep within she knew that her mother was right. He was headed for the nearest bar.

All her hopes and dreams for their home to be like those of other people came crashing down around her. They were going right back to the place they had been three months before.

After a time, Mrs. Cole got control of herself. She stopped crying and went into the bathroom to wash her face and put on new makeup. When she came out a few minutes later, she asked Sandy to go out to dinner with her.

The girl shook her head.

"We'll go to that new little cafe in the hotel. Everybody says it's such a nice place to eat. I guess it's terribly expensive, but they specialize in shrimp and lobster and steak."

"I'm not hungry, Mother."

Mrs. Cole's glance pleaded with her. "I don't want to be alone tonight, Sandy. I don't think I can stand it if I don't have someone to talk to," she said, whining.

Sandy didn't think that she could bear listening to her mother either. "I–I've got a terrible headache. And besides, I don't want to go any place or–or see anybody."

Mrs. Cole's voice grew louder. "It isn't your fault that you've got such a weakling for a father. Nobody will blame you for what *he* does."

Sandy winced. She was angry with her dad because he had gone out, and she was sure he was going to drink again, but she was angry when her mother said anything about it.

"Maybe he won't start drinking," she said hopefully. "Maybe he'll be back in a little while. If we're here, we can talk to him and–and maybe keep him from drinking tonight."

Mrs. Cole stiffened irritably. "So that's why you don't want to go out and eat with me. Well, if that's the way you feel about it, you can stay here. Wait for him if you want to, Sandy. I've waited for him enough to know that he isn't going to come back tonight. He'll be drunk for about two weeks after the fight we had. Then, when he's finally sobered up, he'll come whining back and want me to take up where we left off."

"Maybe things will be different this time."

"Different?" She snorted her indignation. "I'm going out. I'll be back in a couple of hours."

Sandy curled up in a chair in the living room and waited, miserably, hoping her dad would come home, but at the same time realizing that he wouldn't.

If DeeDee were here she would pray for him. She would ask God to keep him from drinking and to bring him home safely and soon. She would pray that God would somehow make all the things right between Mom and Dad again. Sandy longed for her Christian friend.

It was strange how she always wanted to talk with DeeDee when she had any problems. She had a lot of other friends at school, both girls and guys. She knew some of them a lot better than she knew DeeDee. She had known them since she started kindergarten with them. Yet, there was something about her new friend that was different. When she shared some problem or difficulty, DeeDee seemed to understand. She seemed to know exactly how Sandy felt about her parents and especially about her dad. Maybe it was because both of DeeDee's parents were dead, and she had to live with Danny and Kay Orlis. But Sandy seemed to sense that there was more to it than that. At any rate, it was good to have a friend she could confide in.

She got up and went to the telephone. She was just dialing the Orlis number when a car went by slowly. She saw the headlights shining briefly in the front window. Sandy dropped the phone and ran to the window. She was sure it was her dad. It had to be him! He had come driving by to see if there was anyone at home.

He was probably going to come in now and ask her forgiveness and tell her that he had driven over to the bar but had remembered his promise to her that he wouldn't drink anymore, so he hadn't. And if he wasn't drinking, she knew that he and Mom could get things patched up, somehow.

But the car continued down the street. And with it went Sandy's hopes. It wouldn't do any good to think that he wouldn't be drinking. He was probably already in some tavern or liquor store, eyes bloodshot, and his face flushed with alcohol.

Numbly she turned back to the chair. She was weak and trembling inside. Never in all her life had she felt so miserable, so helpless. It wouldn't do any good to call DeeDee. It wouldn't do any good to get in touch with anyone. It was too late for anything to help!

* * *

In their homeroom the following Monday morning, DeeDee looked up as her best friend entered and smiled weakly in greeting.

"Hi, Sandy."

Her friend's eyes spoke to her, but her lips remained silent.

"Sandy!" she exclaimed, keeping her voice low. "Is there something wrong?"

The Cole girl nodded almost imperceptibly. She would have spoken, but her lips quivered until she could say nothing. Without even asking, DeeDee knew what was wrong.

"I'm so sorry." Sandy's smile faded.

DeeDee wanted to go over and talk to her, but that would never do, she realized, not in front of all the other kids. Besides, it was almost time for the bell to ring. Whatever Sandy wanted to tell her would have to wait. It was not until noon that the two girls were able to get together.

Sandy had saved DeeDee a seat away from her other friends in the cafeteria. By this time Sandy was composed enough to talk to her. "I was going to call you last night and have you come over so I could talk to you but I–I couldn't."

"I wish you had," DeeDee replied.

Sandy tried to swallow the lump in her throat. "Oh, DeeDee, it was awful!"

A long, taut silence followed. Since Sandy didn't seem ready to talk, DeeDee prayed silently over her lunch tray. When she finished, she asked, "Would you like to tell me about it?"

Her friend nodded. It hurt even to think about what happened, let alone put it into words. Yet she felt as though she had to share it with someone. And DeeDee was the only one who could possibly understand.

"I–I came home from your place Saturday afternoon, and–" Hesitantly, she began, starting at the time she saw her dad's car in the drive and relating everything that had taken place.

"I thought maybe he would drive around for a little while, and after he got over being so mad would come back, but he didn't. He didn't come home all night or all day or even last night, I don't know where he is or anything."

DeeDee tried to find something encouraging to say to her friend. "He's probably all right. Maybe he went to a hotel somewhere or decided to go to Minneapolis to see about getting a job."

Sandy shook her head. "No, he didn't go out to get a job." She spoke with certainty. She knew her dad too well for that. She had seen him take off on other occasions when he was about to start drinking again. This was exactly the way he had acted. There was no reason for her to believe that this time would be any different.

"Well, you shouldn't believe the worst about him until you know for sure that it's happened."

"And that's not all! Mom has an appointment with an attorney this morning. She says she can't stand living this way any longer. She's filing for divorce!"

DeeDee stared at her friend helplessly. If only there was something she could do to help Sandy. She could only guess how miserable her friend felt, how helpless and alone. At times like this, she wished she were much wiser. "I–I wish there was something that I could do for you," she murmured.

"Thanks, but there isn't anything that anyone can do." Her voice broke. "It's too late for that!"

"Would you like to go home with me tonight and talk with Kay about it?"

Sandy's eyes remained dull and lifeless. "What good would that do?"

"I don't know, but if I had a problem like yours, I think I'd like to talk with someone who's a little older. She just might be able to help you."

Sandy thought about that. She didn't know Kay Orlis very well, but she did like her. And, like DeeDee, there was something about her that inspired confidence. It might be nice to talk to her, but she didn't know whether she could bring herself to do it or not.

"Would she tell anyone?" Sandy couldn't stand that. She would just die if the story got out all over town that her dad was bankrupt and her parents were getting a divorce.

"Kay wouldn't break a confidence, that's for sure."

DeeDee's assurance that Kay would not reveal

any of the information was the deciding factor as far as Sandy was concerned. As soon as school was out, she called her mother and told her that she was going home with DeeDee.

Numbly she went out to the bus with her friend. She was glad she didn't have to go home right then. It wasn't that she didn't love her mother or anything like that. She just couldn't stand hearing her talk about her dad and the divorce and everything else she always complained about.

Kay was at the Orlis home alone in the kitchen when they got there.

"Sandy has something she wants to talk to you about, Kay," DeeDee said.

She dried her hands and followed the two girls into the living room.

Sandy looked around uncertainly. "Will–will Danny and Doug and Del be here?"

"They should be along after a while."

"Is–is there someplace else where we can go?" Sandy's distraught young voice tightened. "Someplace where we can be alone?"

"We can go into DeeDee's room."

In the bedroom Sandy started at the beginning and told Kay everything that had taken place. "And now Mom's getting a divorce," she blurted, "and I don't even know where Dad is."

She had steeled herself to reach that point, and now she began to cry uncontrollably. Kay put an arm around her, holding her close. It was some minutes before the girl was able to stop sobbing. She sat erect, drying her eyes.

"If–if Dad and Mom get a divorce, I won't be able to stand it. I–"

There was a painful silence before Kay spoke quietly. "There is One who can help you through all of this."

Sandy raised her head questioningly. She wasn't exactly sure what Kay meant.

"The Lord Jesus Christ can give you the help you need to get over these difficult days."

The corners of the girl's mouth tightened. "I've prayed and prayed, but it hasn't done any good. Dad's still drinking, and now Mom's going to divorce him!"

Kay's smile showed that she understood. "I haven't gone through anything quite like you're facing, but when I was younger than you are, I lost my father. He died on the mission field in Mexico."

Sandy's expression became sympathetic. "I didn't know that." No wonder you're so understanding, she almost added.

"So I've got some idea of how you feel. But God doesn't promise to work things out the way we want them. Sometimes He works them out in a different way."

Sandy dried her eyes and was listening quietly.

"But He promises to give us the help and strength we need to go through the difficulties that come our way."

The Cole girl choked and began to cry again silently but with sobs that shook her narrow shoulders.

"Right now, Sandy, it's important for you to keep up your courage and to remember that whatever happens, your parents both love you dearly."

"No, they don't." Her lips trembled. "If they did, they wouldn't be getting a divorce."

Kay wasn't sure just how to reassure her about that. She knew that both of Sandy's parents loved her deeply in spite of the trouble they were having, but Sandy could not believe it. To her, the fact that her parents claimed they no longer loved each other was enough to prove that they didn't love her either.

At last Sandy seemed to calm down, and Kay tried to talk with her about her need for the Lord Jesus Christ. But at the moment she didn't seem to be capable of understanding what Kay was trying to say, so great was her bewilderment.

"I hate to ask you this, Mrs. Orlis," Sandy said at last, "but there is something I'd like to ask you to do for me."

"If I can."

"Would you mind talking with my mother about this–this divorce?" It was always hard to say that word.

At first Kay wasn't sure what the girl was asking her to do. "What do you mean?"

"Would you ask her not to divorce Dad?" Sandy was trembling with emotion. "Would you try to get her to give him one more chance?"

Kay hesitated, and Sandy misread it as unwillingness.

"Oh, skip it." The bitterness was back in her voice. "It probably wouldn't do any good, anyway."

"Oh, no," Kay said quickly. "I wasn't hesitating because I wanted to get out of it. I'd be glad to talk with her if I thought it would do any good."

Sandy pleaded with her eyes, desperately. That settled the matter for Kay. She reached out impulsively and took the girl's hand.

"I'll try to talk with your mother, Sandy," she said reluctantly. "I don't know whether it'll do any good, but I'll try."

CHAPTER 3

CONFRONTATION

Sandy Cole wanted Kay to talk with her mother that very evening, but Kay felt that it would be better to wait until she was more sure of how she should approach Mrs. Cole and what she should say.

"I'd like to wait until I've had time to pray and talk with Danny about it," she explained. "We want to have the best possible chance of getting through to your mother when I do talk with her."

Sandy's disappointment showed through, but she agreed that this was probably best.

The following morning, after the triplets had gone to school, Kay took the car and drove over to the Cole home. Sandy's mother came to the door. She seemed genuinely glad to see Kay and invited her in.

Kay followed Mrs. Cole into the kitchen and took a chair at the breakfast nook while Mrs. Cole busied herself making coffee.

"DeeDee is such a dear child. I'm so happy to have Sandy have her as a friend. Sandy needs a close friend – especially now," she added softly.

Kay nodded. "That's what I wanted to talk with you about, Mrs. Cole. Sandy came over to our house last night after school."

Mrs. Cole stiffened. "I might have known. I can't understand what's gotten into that child. She doesn't seem to be able to see any of the faults of that miserable father of hers. He's got her wrapped around his finger until she won't believe that he can do anything wrong."

Kay searched prayerfully for words in the silence as Mrs. Cole poured her coffee into a delicate china cup.

"When Sandy talked with me last night, she was very frank about the things her dad has done."

"I'm surprised at that. Maybe she's finally reached the place where she has to face up to the fact that he's not quite perfect."

Kay ignored the sarcasm in her voice. "Sandy is terribly upset about the trouble between you and Mr. Cole," she continued, "and particularly about the divorce." She looked straight into Sandy's mother's eyes.

The other woman drew herself erect, eyes blazing. "So *that's* why Sandy wanted you to come over and talk with me. Her dad must have put her up to it."

"She hasn't seen her father since he left the house Saturday night."

"He probably called her at school." Mrs. Cole stirred her coffee nervously. "I know him! He'll do anything to get his way. You don't know what a lying schemer he is!"

Without tasting the coffee, she took it to the sink and poured it out, and then she rinsed the cup. With her back to Kay, she went on talking. "You don't know what I've had to put up with. You don't know what it's like to have a man come home drunk and abusive night after night."

Kay prayed for wisdom.

"And now things are even worse!" Mrs. Cole's voice raised. "Do you know what's happened? He's neglected his business so much that he's gone bankrupt. We're losing everything we've got!" She came back and sat down. "I don't know where Sandy and I will go or what we'll do! I'm so worried sometimes I think I'll go out of my mind!"

"I'm sure that–"

Mrs. Cole did not let her finish what she was going to say. "I won't be able to face my friends!"

Kay continued her effort to talk with Sandy's mother, but it was useless. She was so distraught it was impossible to get her to listen to anything. At last, reluctantly, she got up to leave.

"I'm so glad you stopped by. I couldn't talk with my other friends the way I've talked with you. They wouldn't understand."

"If I can be of any help to you, don't hesitate to call me."

Kay had wanted to talk with Mrs. Cole about her need for the Savior. She had wanted to tell her that Christ alone could solve her problems and give her peace, but there had been no chance for that.

Kay was so concerned that she drove out to the airport where Danny was in the hangar working on the plane.

Briefly she related to him what had taken place. "I didn't expect her to be so bitter. I couldn't help her. She wouldn't let me."

"I'm not surprised."

"But what am I going to tell Sandy? How am I going to break the news to her?"

* * *

Sandy went to the Orlis home after school that day and waited impatiently for Kay to come back after talking with her mother. She didn't know what could be taking her so long.

Sandy stood by the kitchen window and looked out on the bleak, snow-hidden yard. She had been doing a lot of thinking the past few days about the trouble that had come between her parents. She finally decided how she could help, but first she had to get the divorce action stopped. Then she would go to her dad and talk to him. He loved her so much he'd do anything she asked him to. She'd get him to promise to stop drinking and gambling and being away from home every night. *Simple as that,* she figured.

It might even help to get her folks to go to Danny and Kay's church. She didn't know why it was, but she didn't think the Orlises ever fought. They laughed and joked around the house, and everybody was happy. And it wasn't like the act her parents could put on for company; it seemed genuine when Danny hugged or kissed his wife.

Sandy saw the Orlis car coming up the lane, and she ran out on the back porch in the chill subzero wind to wait for Kay. A chill more biting than the wind gripped her heart as she saw the serious look on Kay's face and the almost imperceptible sag to her shoulders.

"Did you get to talk to her?"

Kay kicked off her boots and went into the house. "Let's go in here and sit down." It seemed to take forever for Kay to remove her parka, muffler, and mittens and hang them up.

Numbly Sandy followed her into the living room and dropped to a chair across from her.

"She won't change her mind, will she?" Anger and resentment mingled with dismay in the girl's voice.

"You must try to understand your mother's situation, Sandy." Kay chose her words with care. "She has been terribly hurt in ways that you and I can never know, and she's gone through a great deal of heartache and disappointment."

The muscles in Sandy's young face tightened and color drained from her cheeks, leaving them ashen.

"A divorce will only make things worse."

"Your mother has to have a little time to get hold of herself," Kay said. Compassion softened her eyes and brought tears to them. "She's been through a lot and everything's still painfully raw."

"But if we wait, they'll be divorced!"

"I'm sorry."

The girl's temper exploded. "A lot of good that will do!" She drew herself erect and huffed a deep breath. "Well, I can tell both you and Mom right now, I'm not going home! She doesn't love me, and I'm not going to have anything else to do with her!"

"Your mother does love you," Kay told her. "You're all that she has left!"

"And who do I have left?" Sandy asked with venom in her voice. "She doesn't love me!" She said each word distinctly.

"Oh, Sandy, even though you don't agree with what she's doing, you shouldn't talk that way."

Sandy wiped at her angry eyes. She didn't want to admit tears then. "If she loved me, she wouldn't even think about a divorce. I'm not going to stay with her! I don't care what you or anyone else says. I'll run away first!"

"That would only make matters worse."

"They couldn't *be* any worse."

"You're a minor, Sandy. You will have to do what your mother says."

The girl's hostility ebbed slightly, but there was still defiance in her voice. "If Dad can't stay in the house with her, I'm not going to stay there either!"

Kay Orlis did not argue with her, but she was disturbed by the anger and the note of hysteria in Sandy's voice. There was no knowing what a girl like that might do.

Sandy was staring belligerently at her.

"Where will you go, Sandy?"

"I don't know." Her voice was thin and small. "I–I'll try to find Dad, I guess."

"Are you sure he's still in Fairview?"

The girl's voice crescendoed wildly. "Now you sound just like Mom! I suppose you'd be happy, too, if he ran away and I never got to see him again."

"You know I wouldn't be happy about that. And I'm sure your mother wouldn't, either. But I wasn't thinking about where your dad had gone or what he might be doing. I was only concerned about you. You can't strike off on foot looking for someone who's in a car. You'd never find him."

Briefly, fear replaced the anger and defiance. Then she took off on another tangent. "If I can't find Dad, I can find someone else to stay with. I don't have to go where I'm not wanted."

Kay was praying desperately for guidance in knowing what to say to her.

"As long as you don't know where your dad is and you don't want to go home, don't you think it would be best for you to stay here with us?"

Sandy paused, wavering. "And you wouldn't make me go home?"

"I won't *make* you go home," Kay told her, "but if your mother insists on it, there's nothing Danny or I can do about that."

"Then I'll run away!" she retorted, still angry. "I'll run so far she'll never find me!"

"Let me finish!" Kay broke in sternly. "Danny and I will talk to your mother. We'll do everything possible to make her see that it would be best for her to let you stay with us for a little while, but we are going to have to talk to her. We can't be a party to your running away."

Doubt appeared on the girl's attractive young face. "You don't know Mom like I do. She'll want me to be with her because she will be afraid that you'd let me see Dad." She got to her feet and began to gesture with her hands nervously. "If you make me go home with her, I'll run away. Just as soon as I get the chance, I'll leave, and nobody will ever find out where I am!" With that she started to sob once more, uncontrollably. Kay put her arm around her shoulder.

"Don't worry about it, honey. When Danny and I talk with her, she'll understand."

That assurance seemed to satisfy the girl. She stopped crying and even smiled a little.

Kay drove out to the airport where she picked up Danny, and, on the way to town, she told him about Sandy's explosion.

"A lot of kids threaten to run away at one time or another," he said.

"But this sounds different to me. She's desperate enough and confused enough to do almost anything."

They drove straight to the Cole home to talk with the girl's mother. The car was in the drive when they stopped, but it was a long while before Mrs. Cole came to the door. When she did, her eyes were red and swollen. It was obvious that she had been crying most of the time since Kay left earlier in the afternoon.

"There was no need for you to come back. I've made up my mind, and I don't intend to change it. I don't care what you or anyone else has to say!"

She moved as though to close the door, but Danny stopped her. "We didn't come here to get you to change your mind about anything."

"Then you must excuse me. I have a splitting headache, and I don't feel like talking to anybody." She tried hard to keep her expression calm, but the tears in her eyes gave way to anxiety. "This has been a most trying experience for me. I've had just about all I can take."

"And we don't want to add to your burden," he said quickly, "but we do have to talk with you about Sandy."

At the mention of her daughter's name, she flinched. "What's wrong? What's the matter with her?"

"She's all right for now, but we do have a problem."

That broke her anger. She smiled faintly, and stepping back, invited them to come in. They followed her into the spacious living room.

"Now, what is it that's so important about Sandy?"

"You know how upset she is over this divorce," Danny began.

"She just doesn't understand!" Mrs. Cole paced nervously before them. "She seems to think it's my duty to go back to her father. That is all she thinks about. It doesn't matter to her what I've had to go through. Just so I don't leave that precious father of hers! When she comes home, I'm going to make her understand that it doesn't do any good to send anyone to talk to me. The divorce is going to go through!"

"That's just the point," Danny broke in hurriedly. "She doesn't want to come home!"

Mrs. Cole had been facing away from the Orlises. At Danny's words, she gasped and whirled around.

"I hate to have to tell you this, but there's no way I know of softening it. Kay tried for an hour to convince Sandy that she should come home, but she still says that she's not going to!"

Her eyes narrowed, and she folded her arms. "I don't believe it."

"It's true." For the first time since they reached the Cole home, Kay spoke up. "She said that she would run away before she would come back here and stay."

The older woman's eyes flashed. "That's the work of that worthless husband of mine! He's been talking to her! He's been filling her full of stories about me!"

"Sandy hasn't seen her father." Kay spoke with assurance. "I was talking with her this morning, and she told me how concerned she has been about him. She doesn't even know where he is."

"But–but–" Her voice trembled. "She wouldn't turn on me that way. I–I'm her mother!"

"It isn't that she's turning against you, Mrs. Cole. I'm sure of that. Sandy is just upset. She's hurt and confused because she loves both you and her father. She's in terrible emotional turmoil right now."

"I suppose she is." Mrs. Cole slumped in a chair, something she would never permit her daughter to do. "I've been terribly sorry for her. I guess I held off filing for divorce longer than I would have otherwise because of her."

"It's this emotional upheaval that's causing her not to want to live at home right now," Danny explained, leaning toward her with his elbows on his knees and his palms raised upward.

Mrs. Cole eyed him helplessly. "But what can I do?"

"When I talked with her, she did say that she

would be willing to stay at our place," Kay continued, "but we told her that we couldn't give her a definite answer until we had talked it over with you."

At first, Sandy's mother didn't like the idea of having her daughter stay with Danny and Kay. She talked about how lonesome she would be and how badly she needed her at that particular time. It was no wonder Sandy reacted against her mother's selfishness. But, at last, she agreed that it might be best for Sandy to stay with them until she was able to get control of herself. Besides, that would delay her having to cope with the girl herself. Let these people take her if they were so anxious to be martyrs!

"Only I don't want my husband hanging around poisoning her mind against me," she warned.

"The chances are that your husband won't even know where she's staying," Danny informed her.

"Sandy'll tell him if she gets the chance. I know her, and I don't trust her."

When Danny and Kay returned home, the girl was waiting for them, her eyes dark with apprehension.

"She isn't going to let me stay, is she?"

"Oh, yes, she said you can stay with us for a while." Kay's look told Sandy that she was welcome and would be accepted in their home.

DeeDee came in just then and asked Sandy a question about their English assignment for the following day.

"Let me see the book and I'll show you," Sandy answered.

They went into the bedroom together. "I'm so excited I can hardly wait," DeeDee whispered. "What did your mother say? Can you stay with us?"

"She told them I could!" Sandy was speaking in an excited whisper. "They even brought my clothes."

"I'm so glad!"

Then Sandy's face became sad, and she walked slowly over to the window and looked out. "It'll be better than staying at home." Slowly she turned to her friend. "Have I ever told you how lucky you are?"

DeeDee squinted curiously at her. "What do you mean?"

"I used to think that all married couples fight the way my mom and dad used to, but Danny and Kay don't. They get along great." She sat down on a chair near the bed. "I don't know what it is about this house that makes me feel the way I do, but it seems as though I belong here. I feel so–so welcome and content."

DeeDee Davis had always taken for granted their peaceful home situation. "I think it's because Danny and Kay are Christians, for one thing."

But, she thought to herself, *it had to be more than that.* She had been in a lot of homes where the people were Christians and were concerned about living close to God, but she had never been in a home where so many kids liked to come.

CHAPTER 4

THINGS AREN'T SO PEACHY KEEN

In the living room, Doug Davis was talking excitedly to Danny in tones low enough to avoid being heard by the girls in the bedroom.

"What's *she* doing here?" he demanded.

Danny's eyes danced. "Who do you mean?"

"*You* know who I mean, Danny. What's that Sandy Cole hanging around here for?" he asked suspiciously. "What's the deal?"

"You ought to know what she's doing here by this time, Doug," Del broke in. "She just can't resist you."

Doug scowled. "Lay off it, will you?"

With that Danny said, "I don't want you to say anything about this at school or to anyone outside the family, but Sandy has a real problem. She–"

At that moment the bedroom door opened, and DeeDee and Sandy came out. Danny stopped in midsentence.

* * *

The following morning the girls were late coming out of their bedroom for breakfast. Kay noted the time and went briskly to the door.

"You girls'll have to hurry. The bus'll be here before you know it."

DeeDee opened the door and slid out, motioning Kay into the living room. She spoke in a whisper. "I–I've been trying to talk with Sandy." Her voice trembled. "I–I don't know what I'm going to do. Sandy says she's not going to school this morning."

Danny saw there was something wrong and joined them. DeeDee repeated the problem.

"I know how she feels, but she can't stop going to school because she doesn't feel like going. That'll only make it harder for her in the future," he said, shaking his head slowly.

"That's what I told her, but it didn't do any good. She says she's not going and that's all there is to it."

Kay started toward the bedroom, purposefully. Sandy was expecting her and had steeled herself against the visit. She sat stiffly at the dressing table, her eyes cold and expressionless and her mouth clamped shut.

"It's not going to do any good for you to come and try to talk to me. I've made up my mind. I'm not going to school."

"Why not?" Kay's voice was calm, but there was no softness in it.

"You know the answer to that question."

"You can't stay home from school because your parents are getting a divorce, Sandy."

"I wouldn't have to face all the kids." She looked up at Kay through the mirror. Kay could see the desperation in her eyes. "You don't know what it's like, Kay. Everyone in school sits and stares at me."

"DeeDee said she hadn't heard anyone at school talking about it, Sandy. I'm sure you think that because it upsets you so much," Kay said, trying to console her.

But Sandy was not convinced. "I know they're talking about me behind my back. They always do about all the kids. And besides, even if they didn't, I'd still know what they're thinking." She grasped Kay's arm, her fingers tightening about it. "You don't *know* what it's like. They stare at me all the time. I don't care what you say! I'm going to stay at home."

Kay sat down on the bed near her but gave her no sympathy. "All staying home can do is to make things worse."

"They couldn't be any worse!" The words exploded from her lips.

Kay tried to reason with her. "When you've got a difficult situation, the best thing to do is to face up to it. It might be hard for you to go to school for a few days, but if you force yourself to go, you'll find that you'll soon be able to face anyone without difficulty."

The girl's lips were trembling. "You don't know what it's like!"

"That's true enough. But I have had many times in my life when it's been difficult for me to meet people. But I found that the only way to get over it is to face them."

Tears coursed down the girl's cheeks. It was all Kay could do to keep from gathering her into her arms, but at the moment, that would not be wise. Sandy needed stern hands to guide her. Pity would only make her less capable of carrying on alone.

"I'll go this afternoon, but I can't go this morning."

Kay did not relent. "You'll have to go both times. There isn't any choice."

"But I can't!"

"Oh, yes, you can. Now go into the bathroom, wash your face, and come out for breakfast."

For the space of half a minute, Sandy stared at her, shoulders still shaking from her sobbing. She had never felt so sorry for herself in her whole life. Nobody in the whole world understood her or cared. This was more than she could stand!

Kay didn't have any right to order her to go to school. If she was home, Mom would let her stay out of school for half a day if she wanted to. She would probably let her stay home for a week or more. Briefly the temptation to ask to be taken home came over her.

"Sandy! We've talked about this quite enough," Kay continued sternly. "Nothing can be accomplished by going over it again. You have to go to school this morning. Now go in and wash so you can eat breakfast and be ready when the bus stops."

Sandy's lips quivered, and she looked as though she was about to start crying again. "I can't face the kids!"

Kay stood beside the bedroom door, holding it open so the distraught young girl would see that she had not weakened. At last Sandy moved reluctantly toward it. She pushed by Kay and went into the bathroom, still sniffling. A moment later there was the sound of water splashing in the washbowl.

DeeDee came up beside Kay Orlis. "You aren't going to make her go to school today, are you?"

Kay's expression showed determination. "There's no excuse for her staying home."

DeeDee was incredulous. It didn't sound like Kay at all. Usually she was so tender, so understanding. It was as though she didn't think Sandy had any feelings.

"After all that's happened?" DeeDee asked.

"I don't like it any more than you do," Kay tried to explain. "And I feel as sorry for Sandy as you do. But we've got to think about her and what's best for her. It's not going to help her if we let her stay home this morning."

"She promised she'd go this afternoon."

"But this afternoon she'd want to stay at home

again. And if we allow that, what will we do tomorrow morning when she decides that she still doesn't want to go back? I know how hard it is for her to go to school when she thinks all of her classmates are talking about her, but she's got to learn to face them. Believe me, DeeDee, it's the only way."

Sandy came out of the bathroom just then and stormed past Kay, hurt and anger still smoldering in her eyes. She went into the kitchen and sat down. At the breakfast table that morning she said little, but when it was time for the bus to come, she got her coat and went out with the triplets. She and DeeDee walked slower than the boys.

"I didn't know Kay could be so mean."

"She thinks it's best for you to go to school and face the kids."

"I wish she was in my place this morning!" Sandy's anger built. "I'd like to have her know what it's like to have everybody talking about her. Then she wouldn't be so quick to think she knows everything."

DeeDee nodded her sympathy. "I tried to talk to her, but it didn't do any good."

Sandy's lips trembled, and she knew if she spoke, tears would come. The bus came up a moment or two later and they got on, making their way to the back of it.

"I almost wished that I'd stayed home. Mom wouldn't have made me go today. She never makes me do anything I don't want to do."

DeeDee knew that was true. She had been around the Cole home enough the past few months to know that Sandy's mother did let her make her own decisions or, at least, most of them. DeeDee began to wonder if perhaps Kay was deliberately being hard and uncompromising to make Sandy want to go home to her mother. But that didn't sound like Kay either. She could see Kay trying to persuade her friend to go back home, but she would never be mean to her in the hopes that she would decide to leave.

For half a minute Sandy stared out the bus window at the dirty snow piled along the side of the road.

"I sure don't feel like going to school this morning."

"I don't blame you."

"But I'm glad that I'm staying out at your place now and that you're with me. At least I've got someone to talk to." Sandy's head came up and DeeDee caught the wild gleam in her eyes. "If it weren't for you–" she whispered ominously. "If it weren't for you, I'd get off the bus and run as far and as fast as I could run. I'd leave Fairview and never, never, *never* come back!"

"Don't even think about doing anything like that!" DeeDee told her sharply. Sandy wasn't kidding.

"But I can't help it! There are times when I think I can't stand it in Fairview another minute. Right now I'm so confused and upset that I don't think I could even go into that school building if you weren't with me." Tears stood at her eyelashes and while DeeDee watched, they escaped, one by one, and rolled down her cheeks. "I'd run away and never come back!" She turned to look out the window because kids were beginning to stare at her.

"You couldn't do that, Sandy. It could only make things worse than they are already."

Impulsively Sandy reached out and took her arm.

DeeDee eyed her helplessly. She didn't know why, but at that moment, she was more upset about her friend than ever. And the worst thing about it was that she didn't know what she could do to help. She bowed her head and began to pray for Sandy silently.

* * *

Kay was in the living room that afternoon when Sandy and DeeDee came home and got off the bus. Sandy pushed past her frantically and rushed to the bedroom. Kay stared after her. She didn't know whether to follow the girl or leave her alone.

"What's the matter with Sandy?" she asked DeeDee. "Did the kids give her a bad time today?"

"Nothing like that." DeeDee fought back the tears in her eyes. "When we were coming home on the bus tonight, I saw her dad, and before I thought, I pointed him out to her."

"That should have made her feel better. She's been terribly worried about him and has been wondering where he's been."

"That's just it. *She knows now.*" She lowered her voice. "He was in front of a bar, and just as we went by, he went inside."

Kay glanced at the closed bedroom door. That explained it. Sandy knew that her dad was still drinking.

"I didn't mean to make her feel bad, Kay. Honest I didn't."

"Of course you didn't." Her smile was reassuring. "And there's no way you or I or anyone else can keep this sort of thing from happening. It's just one of the problems that Sandy will have to learn to live with."

After a while, Kay went into the bedroom and tried to talk the girl into coming out and having dinner with the rest of the family, but she refused.

"I don't feel like eating." Sobs choked her voice.

"But you have to eat something." Kay was gentle, but insistent. "You'll be sick if you don't."

Sandy started to cry again, silently. It was a minute or two before she could speak. "I–I saw Dad on the street tonight," she said, speaking flatly and without expression, as though there was no life left in her. "He–he went into the bar on Third Street."

Kay nodded. "DeeDee told me."

"Now I suppose Mom will find out that he's still drinking, and she'll be more determined than ever not to take him back."

Kay did not reply. What could she say that would comfort the bewildered, frightened girl?

"I know Dad shouldn't do that, but–" She stopped suddenly. "But how can he help it? She won't even talk to him except to say mean things about him."

Sandy dabbed at her eyes once more with a tissue.

"If I could find him, I know I could get him to promise not to drink anymore." A strange, wistful look gleamed in her eyes. "Do you suppose Danny would take me out to look for him so I can talk to him?"

Kay hesitated. She wanted to do what the girl asked, for Sandy's sake if for nothing else. But she knew what Mrs. Cole would think if Danny did take her to find him. And, after all, Mrs. Cole had the responsibility for the care and guidance of her daughter.

She sat up and leaned forward, pleading with her eyes. "Daddy will do *anything* for me! If I could just find him and talk to him, I *know* he'd promise me not to drink anymore. I just know it!"

Kay fumbled for words, but before she could speak, Sandy continued.

"If I could get him to quit drinking, Mom would stop the divorce and take him back and–and everything would be wonderful again."

"Let me talk with Danny about it," Kay said, hedging.

"But Dad will listen to me!"

Kay had more to say, but she waited until the girl quieted once more. "The most important thing any of us can do now is to pray for him, Sandy. And all of our family has been doing that since we first learned that your parents were having trouble."

Sandy eyed her with amazement. "I–I–" She couldn't speak.

"And I know God is going to answer our prayers."

Sandy's eyelashes blinked the tears away. "Do you really think He will?" It scarcely seemed possible.

"I know He will!"

Momentarily, Sandy thought about that. She had never quite understood what Kay meant about God's answering prayer. She had prayed since she was a little girl. Her mother had taught her, "Now I lay me down to sleep. I pray the Lord my soul to keep. If I should die before I wake, I pray the Lord my soul to take." She still recited that prayer every night before drifting off to sleep, but it really didn't mean anything to her. It was more like another rhyme she had learned as a child, "Twinkle, twinkle little star." The thought of God answering prayer hadn't occurred to her.

Kay sensed what was troubling the girl. "Danny and I have had many, many prayers answered."

"You have?"

"Oh, yes. We go to God with all our problems. And we have been praying for your parents."

Kay was about to talk with Sandy about her need of trusting Christ as her Savior, but the girl was so upset that she felt it would be better to wait for another opportunity before talking with her about her spiritual condition before God. Right then, Sandy didn't need to be told that she was a sinner. The thing to do was simply to show her the love of Christ through their lives.

Sandy came out of the bedroom soon and sat at the table, but she only ate a few bites of food and sipped a little tea. However, when the time came for them to have their evening devotions, she waited eagerly for them to pray for her parents.

Once, while Danny was praying for the Coles, she started to cry. Kay reached over and covered her trembling hands with her own.

As soon as the prayer was over, Sandy went back to the bedroom and closed the door. DeeDee watched her go, sorrowfully.

"I wish there was something we could do for her."

"So do I," Danny said, "but in a mess like this there's very little any outsiders can do."

CHAPTER 5

THE MAN IN THE WOODS

The morning after Sandy Cole saw her dad stagger into the bar, it was obvious that she had slept little the night before. Her bloodshot eyes were swollen, her face was pale, and her hair indicated neglect. DeeDee saw the concern that was indelibly etched on her features. Clumsily she tried to help her friend.

"Kay and I have got a lot of shopping to do. Would you like to go into town with us this morning?"

She tried to make it sound exciting, but Sandy was unimpressed. She shook her head. "I don't think so."

I'm going to look for a new dress."

Sandy's expression still did not change. "I've got a whole closet full of new dresses," she said without enthusiasm. "I don't think I want to go to town." Dejection echoed in her voice. "I don't want to go anywhere, except to go out and look for Dad."

"But you can't sit around the house all the time

without doing anything. Why don't you come to town with me? We'll have a lot of fun."

Her friend stiffened and resentment gleamed in her eyes. "You can save your breath. I'm *not* going to town with you or anyone else. I won't go out where I have to meet people. That's all there is to it! I'm just going to stay home!"

Sandy went back to the bedroom hurriedly, and DeeDee fled to the kitchen to seek Kay's advice.

"I couldn't get anywhere with her, Kay. She won't go to town with us."

Kay wrinkled her forehead. "That's too bad. She really needs to get out a little. We've got to do something to get her mind off herself."

"But how?" DeDee's voice was a plaintive whisper.

Del and Doug came into the kitchen in time to overhear the last exchange. Del had a suggestion.

"If you're talking about Sandy," he said, "why don't you take her horseback riding?"

"I don't think she'd like that."

"She's never been out to see old Barney, has she? She'd like that."

DeeDee's face clouded. "I don't think so."

"How do you know unless you ask her?"

"It might be worth a try, DeeDee," Kay said. "If she's never been in a real Indian home or met an Indian before, she just might want to go."

"That's what I figure. And Barney's a great guy. If she went out to see him once, she'd sure want to go again. If anybody could help her get her mind off her problems, Barney could."

Doug grinned. "I know why you're so excited about that. You want to take her out to see Barney yourself, don't you, Del?"

"Lay off it, will you?"

"That would be a good project for you today," Doug persisted. "She'd just love to have you *show* her around."

"Do you want a punch in the nose?"

"I think she'd enjoy having you for a guide, Del. Want me to ask her for you?"

"You're the one she likes, lover boy."

"I think you're both being just terrible talking that way about Sandy," DeeDee exploded, "when she feels so bad about her parents."

Both boys sobered instantly. "I guess it wasn't very funny," Del said. "I just got carried away when Doug started teasing me about her."

Doug changed the subject. "I really think it would be a good idea to get her to go out to visit Barney if we can." He looked down at his sister. "Do you suppose she'd ride double with you, DeeDee?"

At the breakfast table that morning Del mentioned the old Indian and asked Sandy if she would go out with them to see him. At first she acted as though she was going to turn them down.

"I don't really feel like going anywhere."

"You don't know what you're missing," Del put

in. "Old Barney isn't like any ordinary person, is he, DeeDee?"

"He's great!"

Doug spoke up. "I don't go out there as much as Del does, but I sure do like Barney. You've never met anyone like him. He's really neat."

Sandy paused. "Does he know anything about–about–?" her voice trailed away significantly.

"He doesn't know anything about you or your parents," Del told her, shaking his head, "but it wouldn't make any difference if he did. Barney is one guy who doesn't talk about other people, except to say nice things about them."

There was a long pause. "Well–" She wanted to go and see the elderly Indian and yet she didn't.

"You and I can ride double," DeeDee said. "And if you decide that you want to come home before the boys are ready, we can leave."

"Any time I want to?"

"Any time you want to."

"Okay, but I'm warning you. I might want to leave right away."

As soon as the dishes were done and the guys finished their chores for the morning, they went out and saddled the horses. DeeDee mounted and kicked a foot out of one stirrup so her friend could use it to swing up behind her.

There was a moment's hesitation.

"I've never ridden a horse before."

"You don't have to worry about anything," DeeDee told her. *"She's* gentle."

"For riding double?"

"We've ridden her double lots of times."

As Sandy pulled herself up behind the saddle, Blackie swooped down at them.

"Hello! Hello, Del! Play ball! Run! Run, Doug, run!"

For the first time in days, Sandy laughed.

"Hello! Hello, Blackie." She tried to mimic the crow.

"Hello, Barney! Hello, Del! Strike one! Run, Doug, run!"

"I don't think I've ever heard anything half so funny as that crow of yours, Del."

He tried not to show his satisfaction. "Blackie's a regular clown when he knows that he's got an audience. Just look at him. He knows we're paying attention to him, and he's showing off."

It did, indeed, seem that the crow was aware of the fact that he was putting on a performance for an appreciative audience. He swooped and soared as he chattered to them.

Barney Aubichon hadn't known the kids were coming, but that made no difference to him. He came out to greet them as if he'd been expecting them. His broad smile was as inviting as his voice. "Well, now, Del, I sure am glad to see you. It's been quite a spell since you've been down this way."

"I've been sort of busy." He introduced Sandy to

the old Indian. Barney acknowledged the introduction, smiling and nodding.

"Well now, I sure am glad to know you. I always enjoy meeting any friends of Del's."

Doug snickered and his brother glared at him, but Barney didn't notice.

"Well," he said, "get down and come in. I just might be able to rustle up some cookies to go with the hot chocolate I'm going to make."

At the mention of the food he was going to prepare, Sandy wrinkled her nose distastefully. She didn't know for sure whether she wanted to eat anything he fixed or not, but DeeDee and her brothers didn't seem to hesitate. She couldn't imagine that anything he would prepare could be good, but she had to be polite. She couldn't tell him that she didn't want anything and just leave. Reluctantly she went inside with the others.

The old Indian continued to chatter. "And what brings you out here to see me?" He stood at the doorway while they kicked the snow off their boots.

"You know what usually brings me out here to see you, don't you?" Del asked.

"My cookies?"

"That's one thing."

"I knew it was a mistake when I started feeding you. I suppose I'll never be able to get rid of the likes of you now." Although he tried to sound hard and unfriendly, there was a playfulness in his voice that he could not hide.

"We really came so Sandy could meet you, Barney," Del explained.

The Indian faced her, a kindly gleam in his dark eyes. "Well, now, that was nice of you. That was real nice of you. And I'm right glad to know you, young lady." He looked about as though he suddenly remembered his manners. "I'm sorry I've only got a couple of chairs. You girls take them. I'll get some boxes for the boys and me to sit on."

He came waddling back in a moment or two, carrying three small boxes which he set on end.

"Now, how's that for comfort? You never had it better in your own parlor, now did you?"

Timidly Sandy looked around. She didn't think she had ever been in a cabin quite like this one. It was as neat and as clean as her own home. And that was a surprise to her. She expected the little cabin to be cluttered and very dirty.

But the cabin was so small she found it difficult to imagine what it would be like for even one person to live in it. Her own room at home was twice as large. And Barney's furniture was something else. There was a small, handmade table that showed the marks of the hammer and saw, and two chairs that had been made by the same big hands. Through the open bedroom door she could see an iron bedstead with a thin mattress and a couple of old blankets. Near the head of the bed was an orange crate standing on one end that served as a night table. A Bible laid on it, and another Bible laid on the table at her elbow. Idly Sandy wondered about that. Somehow, she had never thought that an Indian, even an unusual Indian like Barney, would be so interested in Bibles.

Barney started the fire in the airtight heater and put the milk on in a large kettle to heat. "I was just having my Bible-reading when you came. Join me?"

Sandy didn't think much of the idea, but there was nothing she could do about it without making a scene. And she didn't want to do that. So she sat back and listened reluctantly.

He opened the Bible to the book of John where he must have been reading previously and began to read aloud. He didn't find that easy. He stumbled over some of the words, and every now and then he paused and had to start over again. If it had been anyone else, Sandy would have laughed, but she didn't feel like laughing at old Barney. He was too kind, too sincere for that.

When he finished reading, he bowed his head and began to pray slowly as though he was the only one in the room. Only Del knew what to expect. Barney asked God to take care of his family back in Saskatchewan and to bring each of them to Christ. He mentioned his son and daughter-in-law and their children by name, remembering specific needs for each of them.

Sandy didn't know why, but she was thrilled as the old Indian finally mentioned her name, a trace of accent blurring it. It made her feel good just knowing that a man like Barney was praying for her.

CHAPTER 6

TROUBLED TRUCE

Sandy wanted Danny to find her dad and talk with him. He was sure that it would do no good, but the girl was so upset and so anxious that he try that he finally agreed to do so.

"But I'm not sure when I can manage it, Sandy," he said, "or whether he'll listen. I'd have to locate him first and see whether or not he's in a mood to listen."

The hurt gleamed in her eyes. "I'm sure you can find him at one of the taverns or maybe at the hotel where he's staying."

"I'll do my best, but I don't want you to count on my being able to do something that I might not be able to do."

"If you'll just *try!*" she exclaimed in desperation. "That's all I ask."

"I'll try," he promised her.

Danny was driving down Main Street that very

afternoon when he saw Mr. Cole standing in the doorway of a cheap cafe. At first, he wasn't sure that he was actually seeing Sandy's dad. It seemed strange to see a man with his money and position in the community at a place like that. Danny thought he would be more apt to be in one of the more exclusive clubs. But it was an answer to prayer that he saw him at all. Hurriedly, Danny swung over to the curb and parked.

Mr. Cole was still standing near the doorway of the cafe when Danny approached. His hands were thrust deeply into the pockets of his wrinkled suit, and a week's stubble bristled his face.

"Hello there, Mr. Cole."

Sandy's father pivoted to focus his bloodshot eyes on Danny. His cheeks were flushed and bloated, and the odor of stale liquor hung about him like cheap cologne.

Danny saw now why he wasn't hanging out in his usual drinking places. Even if they had allowed him to be there looking as he did, he would have been ashamed to have had his friends and business associates see him.

"Hello, Orlis." There was no friendliness in his voice, but Danny ignored his irritability.

"I was just going by when I saw you. How about having a cup of coffee with me?"

"Sorry. I've got things to do."

"That's too bad. Sandy asked me to come and talk to you."

"Sandy?" His face lit briefly, and he grasped Danny's arm with trembling fingers. "When did you see her? How is she? Does she need anything?"

Danny was pleased at his interest in his daughter. It gave him a starting place, at least.

"She's staying at our place, and except for her concern about you and her mother, she seems to be getting along fine."

"And–and she wanted you to talk to me?" Disbelief crowded into his voice.

Danny nodded. "Let's go in and have a cup of coffee, and we'll talk about it."

Although he had refused to go with Danny a moment before, Mr. Cole now joined him eagerly. They went into the cafe and sat down.

"What about Sandy?" he asked as soon as they had been served. "What did she say? Is there anything she needs or wants?"

"She doesn't need any money if that's what you mean."

Mr. Cole pulled himself up. "You'd tell me if she did, wouldn't you?"

"Of course."

That seemed to satisfy him. He settled back in the booth, still eyeing Danny quizzically. "If she ever needs anything, you'll get in touch with me, won't you? I don't have much left, but whatever I have is hers if she needs it."

"There is something she needs," Danny said

deliberately, "but I don't know if you're prepared to give it to her."

Sandy's dad started to protest angrily but stopped, eyes narrowing. "What are you talking about?"

"Sandy wants a sober father and a home with two parents like the other kids her age."

Mr. Cole snorted. "I'm not the one who's keeping her from having those things, or didn't you know? It's that stupid, nagging mother of hers."

Danny smiled slightly. "Your wife seems to have a different opinion."

"I know that." He was bitter once more. "She's always got a different idea about everything. But I'm giving it to you straight. She's the one who kicked me out. This divorce wasn't my idea!"

"Kay spent a long time talking with her the other day," Danny said. "I think we've both got to be honest enough to admit that you've given her a rough time."

Mr. Cole bristled. "Now don't you go preaching at me. I've had it up to here!"

Danny continued calmly. "I don't believe in divorce for any reason, but I have to be fair and realistic. You've given your wife a lot of trouble, especially in the last few months."

The man's anger died slowly.

"I know." Remorse crept in. He held the coffee cup in both hands and stared into it. "I've been telling myself that same thing over and over again since she filed for divorce. But between you and me, Orlis, it doesn't make it any easier for me to take. I sure didn't want it to end this way."

This much Danny could acknowledge. "But, you know, there is a way you can quit drinking and become the sort of man you want to be."

Mr. Cole put a teaspoonful of sugar in his coffee and stirred it vigorously. "And just exactly what do you know about it? From the way I get it, you've never had a drink in your life."

"That's right, I haven't. But I don't take any particular credit for that myself. The same One who has helped me not to start drinking can help you to quit."

"Now wait a minute!" His temper flared. "It's not as easy as all of that."

"I didn't say it was easy; I said I know the One who can help you."

Mr. Cole's bitterness and self-pity grew.

"Help me? That's a laugh! Nobody can help me!"

Danny paused significantly. "God can help us with all of our problems." He looked steadily at Mr. Cole, without blinking an eye.

Mr. Cole stared coldly back at him, but he remained silent.

"The Bible says–" Danny continued.

He didn't get to finish. The other man gulped his coffee and noisily moved his chair and stood to his feet. "When I want advice, Orlis, I'll ask for it!" His voice was loud enough to carry throughout the cafe.

With that, he pivoted and unsteadily headed outside. Danny stared sadly after him.

What a shame, he thought, *that a life with so much potential should just waste away.* He paid the cashier and went quickly back to his car and headed home. All the way there he wasn't thinking about getting rebuffed or even about Mr. and Mrs. Cole, as unhappy and miserable as they were. He was thinking about Sandy, her pretty, young face sad and her eyes that should be smiling and happy like DeeDee's, dull with bewilderment and frustration.

* * *

Mrs. Cole called Kay several times during the next few weeks to talk with her about her daughter. "I'm so lonely for Sandy, I can hardly stand it. Do–do you think she'll want to come home and stay with me soon?"

Kay hesitated. "I'm not sure, Mrs. Cole. There are times when she seems to be getting her thinking straightened out, and at other times she's as confused and disturbed as ever."

Mrs. Cole sighed. "Have you ever tried to talk to her about coming home?"

"No," Kay spoke slowly. There was still so much anger, so much bitterness in Sandy that her temper flared every time her mother was mentioned. "No, it hasn't seemed wise to talk with her about it yet."

"You aren't trying to win her away from me, are you?" Mrs. Cole asked suspiciously.

Kay's eyes glittered, and her first impulse was to snap back sharply. Mrs. Cole should know the answer to her own question. Kay and Danny had only taken Sandy in to try and help the poor, bewildered girl and her parents. They had provided a home and tried to give her sound counseling in an effort to help her to accept what had happened and to reweave the tattered remnants of her life. They had carefully tried to avoid taking sides or saying anything that might cause her to think less of one parent or the other.

"I'm sorry." Mrs. Cole was contrite now that her own anger had dissipated. "I don't know what makes me say things like that. But I'm so upset, I get to thinking all sorts of wild things. I know you're trying to do what's best for her, and I do appreciate it even though I don't sound as though I do."

"I understand. And I'll try to talk to Sandy about going home as soon as I get a good opportunity to do so. Only don't expect too much from this first visit. It may take her a little while to get used to the idea."

Kay prayed a great deal for Sandy Cole as she did her housework that afternoon. She asked God to help the girl to understand her mother, even though she did not agree with her.

DeeDee and Sandy came in from school chattering loudly about the day's events. Kay motioned

DeeDee away with her eyes. Perplexed, she gathered her books and went into the bedroom to study.

Sandy would have followed her, but Kay asked her to sit down. "I'd like to talk with you for a few minutes, Sandy."

"I suppose Mom asked you to."

Kay did not answer her directly. "What makes you say that?"

"She's called me a lot the last few days and begged me to come back home." She plopped defiantly on a chair near Kay. "I just figured it was about time for her to try to get you to do her dirty work."

"As a matter of fact," Kay said, forming the words with care, "your mother did ask me to talk to you."

"I knew it!" Her voice crescendoed. "I knew it! And she wants you to talk me into moving back home. Right?"

Kay's smile was warm and understanding. It seemed to take some of the fire out of Sandy's manner. "Your mother is very lonely, disturbed, and unhappy, Sandy."

Sandy frowned in irritation. "That's nothing. So am I. And so is Dad."

"And she's terribly lonely for you."

"She should have thought of that before she sued for divorce."

"I have to say that I agree with you about the divorce, Sandy. It would have been much better all around if she hadn't taken that way out. But it's been hard for her too. I'm sure you don't have any idea of what she's had to go through."

Sandy settled back in the chair, the anger in her eyes softening. Her head nodded slightly in agreement. She could remember hearing her dad's drunken cursing and seeing the bruises on her mother's face. What Kay said was true. The last few months had been terribly hard for her mom.

"She wants to do what's best for you, Sandy," Kay continued.

The girl mumbled in reply. "Maybe so, but she's sure got a funny way of showing it."

"Right now, your mother is so lonely she's having a hard time carrying on. She feels that she's been completely deserted."

Sandy clasped her trembling hands. It was not easy for her to talk, but she felt compelled to. "I guess I've been lonely for her, too – as lonely as I've been for Dad."

"I'm sure you have." She waited for a time, allowing the girl to think. "We've enjoyed having you here, Sandy. And both Danny and I agree that you're welcome to make your home with us as long as you want to and it's agreeable with your mother. But I can't help thinking about your mother and how much she needs you."

Sandy's gaze found hers and held there. "What do you think I ought to do, Kay?"

"This is a decision you will have to make."

"I know that, but what would you do if you were in my place?"

Kay hesitated. She didn't want to tell Sandy what to do. It would be much better if she made up her mind without help from anyone else.

"I'd rather not say."

Sandy turned in her chair, crossed her legs, and began nervously kicking her foot. She stared blankly across the room, her eyes focused on some distant horizon. At last, she spoke. "If I did go back home, Mom would probably start saying all those terrible things about Dad again. And I just can't stand it, Kay!"

"We could talk with her about it first, if you'd like."

Sandy faced Kay. "Would you do it for me, Kay? I couldn't stand it if I had to listen to that all the time."

"Of course, I will."

Kay saw Mrs. Cole that afternoon and explained the situation with Sandy to her.

"I don't know why she keeps defending that no-good dad of hers," the older woman retorted bitterly. "It's always been that way. Since she was a little girl, he's been able to wrap her around his little finger. She'd do *anything* he wants her to."

Kay went back over her conversation with Sandy again, explaining the girl's reason for not wanting to come home.

"Sandy's trouble is that she loves both you and her father very much, and it hurts to hear one of you talk about the other."

Mrs. Cole was indignant. "I think I've been most restrained in anything I've said about that husband of mine, but I can see Sandy's position, and I certainly don't want to hurt her any more than she's been hurt already."

"That's exactly what I told her this morning. I said that I knew you would agree to stop talking about her father in front of her if you understood how much it hurts her."

Mrs. Cole wanted Sandy to come back that very afternoon, but she insisted on waiting until the next day. She and DeeDee had some studying to do, she said, and they wanted to do it together. To Kay, she confessed a different reason.

"I know I promised that I'd go back home, but whenever I think about it, I freeze inside. I don't know what's the matter with me."

"I know how you feel, but I'm sure everything is going to be fine between you and your mother now. She's promised not to talk about your dad in front of you." Kay smiled. "And that ought to make being home with her much more pleasant."

"*If* she keeps her promise," Sandy continued doubtfully. "But I know what's going to happen. Everything will be great until she gets me home with her. Then she'll start in on Dad again." The girl's voice sharpened. "And, Kay, if she does it, I won't stay there! I'll run away!"

Kay listened with growing uneasiness. What

Sandy said was all too likely to be true. It wouldn't be that Mrs. Cole wouldn't want to keep her word. She fully intended to. But with her, intending to do something and doing it were two different things.

And Sandy was desperate enough to do something foolish if her mother kept up a bitter tirade against her dad. It was such a hard situation and so confused and bewildering. Kay found it affecting her own life, and she wasn't personally involved in it.

The next afternoon Mrs. Cole came over to the Orlis home and waited for her daughter. Sandy seemed glad when she saw her. She flew into her arms.

"Oh, Mom!"

Their tears flowed unchecked.

CHAPTER 7

A GOOD SCARE

Sandy Cole and her mom went out to a quaint little restaurant for dinner that night. Sandy would have preferred going right home, but her mom wanted to show her the new eating place she had found.

"It's a little expensive, but I thought we should celebrate tonight, and it's such a charming place. After all, this is something of an occasion for you and me, isn't it?"

"Yes, Mom." They were shown to a table in a far corner.

"I'm so glad you decided to come home." Mrs. Cole was in one of those cheerful, talkative moods in which the words gushed out. "It seems as though it's been ages and ages since we've been together."

Sandy murmured her assent. She pretended to be engrossed in the menu.

"You don't know how many nights I've cried myself to sleep since–" She caught herself just in time. "Since you've been staying with the Orlises."

"I know." Sandy had been doing the same thing herself.

Mrs. Cole eyed her narrowly, as though she couldn't possibly understand, but she did not say what was on her mind. "But anyway, you're back home with me now, and that's all that matters."

Sandy tried to change the subject by asking what she should order, but her mother wanted to continue the conversation.

"There's something I've been wondering about, Sandy."

"Yes?" There were warning signals in her voice.

"Have–have you seen your dad since–since you've been staying with Danny and Kay Orlis?"

Sandy stiffened. "Mom! You promised!"

"I didn't say anything about him," she answered defensively. "I only asked if you'd seen him. Is there anything so bad about that?"

Sandy picked up her fork, fingered it nervously, and laid it down once more. "No, I haven't seen him. Now, *please* can we talk about something else?"

Mrs. Cole stared at her helplessly.

"I don't know what's so terrible about my asking a simple question about your father. After all, I was married to him for twenty years."

"*Was* married to him." Sandy's bitterness seemed

to intensify. "But you're not married to him now. You're divorced. Remember?"

Mrs. Cole flinched. "You make it sound as though I've got leprosy or something."

Sandy leaned forward, tears clinging to the tips of her eyelashes. "Mom, please! I want to be home with you, but I can't stand it if you keep talking this way."

"All right." Mrs. Cole drew herself erect. "If you want to change the subject, that's all right with me. What do you want to talk about?" Her feelings were hurt by Sandy's outburst, and she was determined to let her know about it. Her philosophy was, when I suffer, I won't do it alone. As a result, she had given both Sandy and her father giant guilt complexes.

The happy mood of the earlier part of the evening was shattered. They made half-hearted attempts at conversation, but there were long periods of silence, and not even their lobster dinners created any enthusiasm.

They drove home in silence. Sandy carried her clothes upstairs and hung them in the closet. Mrs. Cole stayed downstairs, trying to get interested in a new mystery novel. Before they went to bed, Mrs. Cole came into Sandy's room, the hurt still showing in her eyes.

"I'm sorry about tonight, dear."

"I'm sorry too, Mom." Her smile indicated she was trying to understand and forgive her mother. "It's all right."

"I don't mean to keep saying things like that."

"I've already told you! It's all right!"

Mrs. Cole went over and opened the closet door.

"You know, I was just thinking, you haven't had any new clothes for a long time."

"I don't need any new clothes." She really didn't mean that. She always liked to get new clothes, but she didn't like the idea of having her mother try to bribe her by offering to buy her something.

"I've never seen you when you didn't need new clothes." She brushed Sandy's protest airily aside. "How would you like to go shopping Saturday?" Mrs. Cole asked enthusiastically.

"Shopping?" She weighed the word briefly. "What for?"

"Oh, whatever you'd like to have. I thought it would be nice to get you a new spring coat, a dress or two, and some shoes. They have the loveliest things at Millie's."

"It sounds nice, but I don't really need anything, Mom."

"That doesn't make any difference." Her laughter was forced. "I just feel like going on a little shopping spree and thought you might like it, too. How does that sound to you?"

Sandy hesitated. "What about the money?"

Sandy had never before thought about where money to buy new clothes would come from, but she had just spent several weeks with Danny and

Kay where money wasn't as plentiful as it had been in her home. They usually had to talk over their purchases. And sometimes they had to wait a week or two before getting what they needed. That had made Sandy more conscious of money.

She was also dimly aware of the fact that the law would probably set the amount of money her mother would get from her dad now that they were actually divorced. It was called alimony. So now her first consideration was how much the shopping trip would cost.

"Money? I'm not going to worry about money as long as my credit cards hold out."

In spite of the excitement of getting new clothes, Sandy felt bewildered and dejected as she got ready for bed.

It all began with an idle thought. She was about to switch off the light when she remembered that the last time she had slept in her own bed was shortly after her mother had filed for divorce. She had lain awake half the night worrying about where her dad was and what he was doing.

Now she didn't know the answer to either of those questions, but she was afraid he was drinking and gambling the same as always. If she could only see and talk to him! A sob choked in her throat. Now that the divorce had become final, she might never see him again.

Sandy was crying when she went to bed and was still crying when she finally drifted off to sleep.

* * *

Sandy didn't say anything to her mother about it, but she had gone to Sunday school and church when she stayed with Danny and Kay. Now that she was home, she felt a strange uneasiness the following Sunday morning. It was time for church, and she couldn't sleep. At last she could stand it no longer, so she got up and dressed. She poured herself a glass of orange juice and drank it slowly, sitting at the breakfast nook. It was almost noon when her mother came downstairs.

"Oh, you're up," she remarked as she saw her daughter. "I didn't expect you to be out of bed on Sunday morning at this hour."

The girl did not look up nor turn to face her. "I couldn't sleep."

Her mother came over to her and would have gathered her into her arms, but she was stiff and unresponsive. "Is there something wrong?"

No answer.

"What is it, darling? Tell your mom."

Sandy was embarrassed, but she had no choice but to answer her mother's insistent questions.

"I would have liked to have gone to Sunday school and church this morning, that's all."

Mrs. Cole beamed knowingly. "Of course. I might have known that you would want to show off your new clothes to your friends today. I don't know why

I didn't think of it." She glanced at her watch. "I'm sorry I stayed in bed so long that you didn't get to go."

Sandy felt herself wither inside. Her mother didn't understand at all. The fact didn't occur to her that Sandy might want to go to church because she felt she needed spiritual help.

"I'll tell you what we'll do. I'll hurry and get dressed, and we'll go out to that little restaurant we were at the other night. A lot of our good friends eat there. You can wear that adorable burgundy voile dress and your new pink shoes. It will be almost as good as going to church."

"No, Mom!" Sandy tried to sound pleasant and agreeable, but there was a harshness to her voice.

But Mrs. Cole was already on her way upstairs.

"Hurry and get dressed, Sandy, or we won't be able to get a table," she called over her shoulder. Her bedroom door closed on her last word.

Resignedly, Sandy went upstairs and began to change clothes. It was easier to do what her mother wanted her to do than to argue with her.

On the way out to the cafe they drove past the corner where Sandy had last seen her dad. Although the bar was closed and the street was empty, she could still visualize him standing there, hands thrust deeply in his pockets and dejection in every move. It was all she could do to keep from crying.

Her mother noticed that she had grown suddenly quiet and tried to find out the reason, but Sandy wouldn't tell her anything.

Somehow, they were able to get through the rest of the day without arguing. That night she thought again about going to church. Danny and Kay and the Davis triplets even went to church on Sunday evenings. *But it wouldn't do any good to talk to Mother about going,* she reasoned. She might go to her own church on Sunday morning, but she would never go to Danny and Kay's church, especially on Sunday night. So they sat and watched television.

Sandy only half saw the programs. The other half of her mind was hunting for her dad, trying to think where he could be or what he was doing. It didn't seem right for them to be sitting there enjoying themselves when he might be hungry and cold or even sick.

The next morning when Sandy came down for breakfast, it was obvious that she had been crying. Her eyes were bloodshot and swollen and dejection was written all over her face and made her shoulders sag. Mrs. Cole gasped as she looked at her.

"Sandy!" She rushed over to her. "What is it? What's wrong?"

The girl pushed past her into the kitchen.

"What is it, Sandy? Answer me!"

"I'm all right! Just leave me alone!"

"You certainly don't look all right! Are you still moping around because I kicked that worthless dad of yours out of the house?"

Sandy's gaze came up defiantly. "Mom, I'm warning you!"

"And I'm warning *you,* young lady! I've had all of this nonsense I can stand! I'm not going to keep talking about that drunken bum who's your father, but you've got to do your part, too. You go around as though you've just come from somebody's funeral. I want it to stop! I want to have a good time with you."

Tears washed narrow paths on Sandy's cheeks, but the girl said nothing. When she finished eating, she started to her room. By this time, Mrs. Cole was sorry for her outburst.

"I'll take you to school this morning, honey."

Sandy stopped on the stairs and pivoted deliberately. "I can't go to school today, Mom. I feel terrible."

She thought that would end the matter. Her mother had always allowed her to stay home before when she wanted to, but this time she insisted that Sandy go to school anyway.

"I know exactly how you feel, but you can't stay at home. The principal will take something off your grades if you miss any more school."

"But I can't go! I'm sick. You wouldn't make me go to school if I'm sick, would you?"

"You don't look sick to me. Now go up and wash your face and put on some makeup. I'm going to drive you to school."

Sandy continued to protest, but it was useless. Her mother refused to listen. At last she realized she was not going to succeed and did as she was told. Her mother got the car out of the garage and drove her across town to school.

Sandy opened the car door and started to get out.

"I can't do it, Mom," she protested. "I can't go in there and face the kids."

"You don't have anything to be ashamed of. If it was your father, he might have some reason to hang his head and try to avoid people, but you and I don't have to feel bad. Everyone knows that what we've done has been because of the way he's treated us. Everyone knows where the real trouble comes from."

"I can't help it, Mom. All the kids look so funny at me! I can't face my old friends or anyone."

"Nonsense!" She started to cry, too. "Please, Sandy, don't give me any more trouble. Do as I say!"

Numbly, the girl got out of the car and started in the direction of the school. Her mother pulled slowly away from the curb and turned at the next corner.

Mrs. Cole couldn't figure out what was wrong with her daughter. Sandy wasn't herself anymore. Usually she was such a happy, carefree girl. And she used to love school. She hadn't wanted to stay home even when she was really ill. And last spring she had been on the honor roll. But now her grades were dropping drastically. Mrs. Cole hadn't felt that she could talk with Sandy about it, but only the week before the principal had called to tell her about it.

"I don't understand what's happened to Sandy the last few months," he said. "She isn't interested in her studies anymore. Frankly, Mrs. Cole, she's doing failing work in two subjects, and that isn't like her at all."

Mrs. Cole had promised to talk with Sandy. She thought she knew the reason for the trouble. It was Sandy's dad and his drinking. If only he hadn't allowed himself to get so far gone with liquor, Sandy wouldn't be having the trouble she had now. Mrs. Cole had thought of that while she was talking with the principal, but she didn't feel free to tell him, in case he hadn't heard about the divorce.

She still didn't know how she was going to get to talk to Sandy about it. The girl was so touchy about everything. Mrs. Cole was afraid Sandy would get mad if she even mentioned her low grades. But she had to think of something. She was still considering the matter when her phone rang. It was the principal's secretary.

"This is Miss Larson at the high school. I'm calling to see if Sandra is ill. She didn't come to school this morning."

"She–she didn't?" Mrs. Cole's head swam. She had taken her daughter to school herself and let her out. "There must be some mistake."

"She's been reported absent in her first two classes this morning."

Mrs. Cole didn't know what she had said then. She sat down on a chair nearby as soon as she hung up. Sweat beaded her forehead, and her hands began to shake.

What happened to Sandy?

CHAPTER 8

TROUBLE ON TOP
OF TROUBLE

For a time after she hung up, Mrs. Cole held the phone, tears swimming in her eyes and her shoulders shaking with fright. She had been afraid something like this was going to happen sooner or later. And there was nothing she could do about it. Her daughter wasn't in school. She was gone! Maybe she had run away.

Self-pity engulfed the girl's mother. What was happening to Sandy, anyway? Why would she do a thing like this? Didn't she realize what she was doing to the one person who loved her more than anyone else in all the world?

Even as Mrs. Cole posed the question, the answer came. Sandy was probably trying to get back at her, to make her suffer for not dropping the divorce action and taking her dad back. She was probably out at

Danny and Kay's enjoying herself and not caring at all that her mother was almost beside herself with worry.

It wasn't like Sandy to play hooky from school, she said inwardly. *That father of hers must have influenced the girl.* If it weren't for something like that, Sandy would never have stayed away from school and caused her to worry. That sort of thing just wasn't like her daughter. She was more considerate than that.

Once Mrs. Cole convinced herself that her husband was influencing Sandy against her, she was able to control her emotions. She dried her tears and called Kay. She had been certain Sandy was out at the Orlis place, but Kay said that she hadn't seen her since she moved back home.

"Isn't she in school?"

Mrs. Cole's voice tightened. "I can't understand it. I took her to school myself. But the principal's office called a little while ago and wanted to know if her absence was caused by illness."

Kay fought a numbing dread that threatened to engulf her. It had only been a short time before that Sandy had indicated she was thinking of running away. Kay thought she had talked her out of it – until now.

"I'm sure that husband of mine – that *former* husband – put her up to this. Sandy has always been an obedient child. She would never do anything like this on her own."

Kay did not reply, except to assure Mrs. Cole that she would phone at once if Sandy did return to the

Orlis home. "And you'll call me as soon as you hear from her, won't you, Mrs. Cole?"

"Of course." Her gratitude was apparent. "I want to thank you and your husband for the help and encouragement you've given me." She faltered. "I don't know what I'd do if it weren't for friends like you two." She started to cry once more.

Kay hung up the phone thoughtfully. She and Danny were concerned about the Coles and wanted to help them, but they seemed so hard, so unconcerned, so unreachable with the love of Christ and so immune to the gospel.

The day plodded ponderously on for Mrs. Cole. Each minute was an hour, each hour a week. She tried to make herself believe that everything was all right, that there had been an error in the school records in spite of what the principal's secretary said and that Sandy had been in school all the time.

But, as the time crawled by, she was sure that was not the case. One teacher might make such an error, but not all of them would report Sandy absent if she was actually in classes. Impatiently Mrs. Cole watched the clock, trying to decide what to do. How long should she wait before she called the authorities? And if she did, what would she tell them?

It was shortly after four o'clock, and Mrs. Cole was on the telephone once more calling Danny and Kay's number when the front door opened and there was a familiar step on the carpet.

"Sandy?" Her voice was trembling. "Sandy, is that you?"

Sandy sauntered into the kitchen where her mother was standing, holding the phone.

"Who'd you expect?" Sarcasm sharpened her young voice. She was chewing gum obnoxiously, as if daring her mother to reprove her for it. Mrs. Cole ignored the gum in her relief to see Sandy.

"Where have you been?"

"That's a stupid question." Sandy sat down. "I've been at school. Where else?"

Mrs. Cole stared at her. Sandy was lying! For the first time – that she knew about – her daughter was lying to her!

"Sandy Cole," she said, her voice abrasive, "you've lied to me. You aren't telling me the truth."

Sandy's cheeks flamed, but she did not admit that she had lied to her mother.

"Who told you that I lied to you?" She tried to keep her tone controlled, but it didn't work. "You know I don't tell you things that aren't true!"

Mrs. Cole took her daughter's hands in her own. "Don't say that, Sandy. Don't make it worse!"

The girl's lower lip trembled. "If you'd rather believe someone else than your own daughter, all right. I won't even try to make you believe me. Go ahead. Think I'm a liar."

Mrs. Cole began to cry again. "Sandy, I *know* you didn't tell me the truth. You weren't in school today."

"Who said I wasn't?"

"The principal's office." She spoke reluctantly, as though the telling added to Sandy's guilt. "They called this morning to see if you were ill."

Sandy stared at her mother, then turned quickly away. "I–I–"

"Where were you? What were you doing?"

She pressed her lips together for a moment, then said, "I *told* you that I couldn't go to school today. I told you that I couldn't face the kids."

Mrs. Cole's temper kindled. "But you promised that you would."

"I didn't promise anything." Her manner was defensive. "You asked me to go to school, but I didn't say that I would." Sandy went to the living room and turned on the television. Mrs. Cole followed her in and turned it off. For a minute, they stood glaring at each other. Then Mrs. Cole crossed to the couch and sank heavily onto it. "I don't know what's wrong with you or why you insist on being so difficult." Her lips quivered. "I'd think you would be considerate enough of me and all I've been through to want to do at least *some* of the things I ask. You know how upset I've been lately!"

Sandy stared at her angrily but did not reply.

"Why did you do this to me?" Her mother's voice crescendoed. "Just answer me, Sandy! Why?"

"Why did you do what I asked you not to do, Mom?"

"And what did you ask me not to do?"

"Go ahead with that divorce!"

There was a long, breathless silence. Mrs. Cole stifled an anguished sob. "That's all the thanks I get from you. I try to be a good mother to you. I buy you anything you want. But what thanks do I get? This!" She gestured wildly with her hands. "You lie to me!"

Sandy started to cry silently, holding her hands over her face. Her mother's voice was low.

"Is it too much to ask where you've been all day?"

Sandy lifted her head. "Around."

"Did you see your father?"

"No!" She spat out the word. "But I would have if I could've found him! You might just as well know that right now."

Mrs. Cole squinted at her incredulously, as though unable to believe Sandy's outburst.

"You weren't out looking for *him!*"

It was hard for Sandy to speak, but when she did, her voice rasped like sandpaper over soft wood. "Would it make any difference if I was?"

Mrs. Cole got up slowly, started to cross the room, and then came back once more. "Where did you look?" she demanded. "You didn't go into those awful taverns, did you?"

"I went into the taverns *and* the liquor stores *and* the bottle clubs." Sandy's tears boiled over, and anguish shook her slight, young frame. "I went every place I could think of, but I couldn't find him anywhere."

* * *

The next three days were strained and uncomfortable at the Cole house. Sandy said very little to her mother, except in answer to her direct questions. After a few attempts to get her to talk, Mrs. Cole lapsed into an injured silence. She, too, spoke only when it was absolutely necessary. Neither of them mentioned Sandy's being absent from school, but it was never far from their minds.

Mrs. Cole insisted on taking Sandy to school and coming after her in the afternoon. The girl didn't like it and tried to argue with her mother, but it was useless. She insisted on doing it.

"You said yourself that you didn't like the idea of being around the kids at school any more than you absolutely have to."

"But–" How could she tell her mother that she resented being treated like a baby? How could she blurt out the truth that she didn't like not being trusted? But it did no good trying to talk to her. She never listened anyway.

They were just driving into the yard on Friday afternoon when a car pulled in behind them.

"Who's that?" Mrs. Cole asked.

"Why, it's Sheriff Riley! I wonder what he wants."

"It probably has something to do with that worthless father of yours." She muttered under her breath, but Sandy heard her and winced. The sheriff came over and spoke to them.

"Could I have a word with you, Mrs. Cole?"

She smiled. "Of course. Won't you come in?"

"I don't have time for that. I just came to leave these papers with you."

She stared at them with horror.

"What are they?"

"They're from the loan company that holds the mortgage on your house. Your husband hasn't been making payments on it, and they're foreclosing."

Sandy watched her mother's reaction as Mrs. Cole gasped aloud. She didn't know what it meant, but it didn't sound good.

"What's this all about, Mom?"

It was some time before she could speak again.

"It–it's the house! Your father hasn't been making the payments, and they're going to take it away from us!"

They made their way into the house numbly and sat in the living room facing each other. "There's some mistake, isn't there, Mom? They aren't *really* going to take our house away, are they?"

Mrs. Cole nodded. "Those papers said they are going to sell it. We'll have to move out."

Hysteria crowded into Sandy's voice. "But where will we go?"

"I don't know where! All I know is that your dad has ruined everything for us. We've got to move."

Sandy was folding and unfolding her hands nervously.

"I was to get the house and your father was to make the payments," she continued. "That was part of the divorce settlement. But he hasn't done it! That's why they're taking it away from us!" Her voice broke. "I'm going to see my attorney. Your father is going to jail!"

Sandy Cole caught her breath sharply. "You–you wouldn't do that!"

"Oh, wouldn't I? You just wait and see!"

CHAPTER 9

THE RUNAWAY

Sandy Cole stared at her mother, her eyes wide with fright. "You don't really mean that!" she exclaimed. "You aren't going to have them put Dad in jail!"

Mrs. Cole's eyes were blazing. "I most certainly am. He doesn't need to think that he can pull a rotten trick like this on me and get away with it!"

Sandy was numb. This wasn't her mother talking. She was gentle and kind. This was a stranger, bitter, hostile, and vindictive. But the familiar voice went on, grating harshly on her ears.

"This is just like that father of yours! He never thinks of anyone other than himself. I should have known something like this would happen. He's done it purposely!"

"I know he hasn't, Mom," Sandy said defensively. "He isn't that kind at all. He wouldn't do that to us!"

"But he *has* done it to us! You saw the sheriff; you heard what he said. We're losing the house. Now we don't have any place to live! We're being thrown out on the street."

Sandy moistened her lips. The same fear that gripped her mother tightened its vice-like hold on her. Where would they go? Where would they live?

"Do–do we have to move right away?" she asked.

Desperation replaced the anger that was flaming in her mother's face. "I don't know." She pulled in a thin breath and expelled the air slowly. "I don't know."

Sandy was helpless. If only there was something she could do, something that would make it possible for them to continue to live in their home.

Her mother had been motionless for the last several minutes. Now she got to her feet and headed resolutely for her upstairs bedroom.

"Where are you going?" Sandy wanted to know.

"I'm going to change clothes and go down to my attorney's office. I'm going to file a complaint against your father. He'll find out that he can't treat us this way and stay out of jail!"

Sandy sank weakly to the chair. Her mother always talked a lot and made all sorts of threats about what she was going to do if she didn't get her way. Usually Sandy didn't pay much attention to her when she was so mad. But, instinctively, Sandy realized that her mother wasn't going to change her mind. She was going to do exactly as she said she was.

She forgot her concern over where they were going to live. The only thing that mattered now was that her dad was going to be arrested and put in jail, and there was nothing she could do about it.

It was shortly after five when Mrs. Cole reached the attorney's office. He was gone and the office was closed.

Mrs. Cole rattled the door impatiently, hoping he was still inside and would come and open it. She couldn't understand why he had to leave so early. It seemed as though he had done it purposely to irritate her. Now she would have to wait until the following Monday to prefer charges against that exasperating man.

She stood at the door for a moment or two, trying to decide whether or not to phone the lawyer at home. In one way she wanted to get him working on the matter as quickly as possible. But she had to admit that it probably wouldn't do any good to see him away from the office. He would have to make out the proper papers and send them to the courthouse or call the sheriff or whatever it was that had to be done in such cases. There wasn't time to do anything until Monday morning.

She started slowly back to her car. If she went home now, she would have to face her daughter's tearful pleading for her to change her mind. And that was something she wanted to avoid. Her husband knew what that house meant to her. The least he could have done was to have kept up the payments. And if he had thought anything of her and Sandy, he would have.

No, it didn't make any difference how Sandy pleaded, she wasn't going to change her mind. She would see that he got what was coming to him.

Mrs. Cole was still debating whether to go home and face Sandy or postpone it for a time. As she neared the house, she made up her mind, turning and heading for the new little cafe she found so charming. She'd go out and eat while she worked out what she was going to tell her daughter. Somehow, she had to make Sandy see that having her father arrested and prosecuted was the only way to solve their problem.

It was almost eight o'clock when she finally drove back home, feeling no better or more sure of herself than she had when she found the attorney's office locked. When she was a block from home, she saw that there were no lights on in the house. *Sandy must be watching television,* she decided. Otherwise, she would have at least one room well lit.

Mrs. Cole swung into the drive and got out hurriedly. She didn't know why, but a vast uneasiness swept over her – an uneasiness she could not explain. She ran to the front door and flung it open.

"Sandy!" Her voice rang resoundingly through the house. "Sandy!"

The silence was deafening.

"Sandy!"

She checked the urge to call her daughter's name

once more and switched on the light. There was no reason to get so upset. Sandy probably left a note saying where she had gone and when she would be back. That was one of the things she always appreciated about her daughter. Sandy had never been a worry to her.

But there was no note in the living room. The older woman straightened thoughtfully, trying to figure out what Sandy would have done. She usually went out the back door. The note was probably in the kitchen.

There was an envelope on the table, she saw with relief. She shouldn't have let herself get so upset. Nevertheless, her fingers were trembling when she opened it and extracted the folded sheet of paper.

Dear Mom–

I can't stand to stay here and see Daddy go to jail.

I'm sorry.

I love you,

Sandy.

Mrs. Cole's hand shook until the note slipped from her fingers and fluttered to the floor.

Sandy had run away!

Scarcely realizing what she was doing, Mrs. Cole picked up her phone and dialed Kay Orlis.

"Hello," she said breathlessly, "is Sandy there?"

Kay didn't even recognize her, her voice was so charged with emotion. "I'm sorry. You must have the wrong number."

Then Mrs. Cole quieted herself enough to tell Kay who she was.

"No, I haven't seen her for two or three days. Is there anything wrong?"

It was a full minute before the older woman was able to speak. "She's run away."

"No!" Fear choked Kay's voice. That was what she had been dreading, what she had been praying would not happen!

Kay remained motionless for a moment or two, still holding the telephone with a trembling hand. The muscles in her face were taut, and her gaze was fixed and glassy. Danny, who had heard her side of the telephone conversation and had seen her concern, went over to her.

"What's wrong?" he whispered.

The sound of his voice seemed to jar her. She started suddenly and faced him.

"That was Mrs. Cole." Her voice was flat and expressionless. "Sandy Cole has run away."

"Is she sure?"

"She left a note."

They went back to the living room and sat down. "I've been afraid that was going to happen, and I can't say that I'm surprised. A person doesn't have to be around her very long to know that she's upset enough over this divorce to do most anything."

Kay nodded. "For the last month I've tried to get Mrs. Cole to see that Sandy is all upset and that she ought to be careful what she said to her."

Danny finished the statement. "But she's too preoccupied with her own problems to think about anyone else."

"That's right."

Danny thought about Mrs. Cole and the problems that she had faced in the last few months. Although he didn't agree with the action she had taken, he had to admit that she had more than enough provocation to do something.

"I can't help feeling sorry for her."

"Neither can I," Kay replied, "but I feel even more sorry for Sandy. She's caught in the middle between her parents."

"And she can't do a thing about it."

After a short pause, Kay continued. "Mrs. Cole seems to think that her husband is responsible for Sandy's running away. She told me that Sandy has always been an obedient girl and that she wouldn't have run away unless someone else talked her into it."

"I think she's mistaken about that. Sandy's one mixed-up kid right now. I'm sure she isn't even thinking straight. That's what makes this so serious. But it's no use to tell her mother the way we think. That would only make her more upset than ever." He got to his feet and paced the room, suddenly as nervous as Kay. "Did Mrs. Cole say whether she called the police?"

"I'm not sure, but she talked as though she was going to if she hasn't already."

He came back to stand before her.

"You know Sandy a lot better than I do, Kay. Where do you think she could have gone?"

Kay shook her head. "That's hard to say, but she may have gone out to see if she could find her dad."

"I was thinking the same thing myself." He went to the hall closet and got his sweater. "I think I'll make the rounds of the taverns in town to see if I can locate anyone who's seen her since dinner tonight."

"I wonder–"

Kay Orlis was interrupted by a brisk knock on the door. Danny was surprised to see Sheriff Riley standing there.

"Hello, Sheriff. Come in."

"I can only stay a minute." The officer stepped in on the rug, holding his hat in his hand.

"What brings you out this way?"

"I'm sorry to bother you, but Mrs. Cole called a little while ago about her daughter. Apparently, she's run away."

"We know. She called here, too."

"I'm not surprised," the sheriff went on. "The poor woman's beside herself. Everything seems to be happening to her these days."

There was a hint in the officer's voice that he was only telling part of the story, but neither Danny nor Kay questioned him about it.

"The report that Sandy is missing went out on both television and radio a few minutes ago, and we had a phone call that she was seen heading this direction, so I came out to check."

Danny told the officer he would phone him immediately if she should come to their house. Sheriff Riley thanked him and started away. He was almost to the edge of the porch before he turned and came back.

"Do you know where Mr. Cole is?" he asked.

Danny Orlis shook his head. "I haven't seen him for two weeks or more. In fact, I was just getting my sweater to go out and look for him. There's a possibility that he might know where she is, the way I see it."

"I've got the local police checking the beer joints and liquor stores. If he's in town, they should find him that way."

With that he was gone. As soon as he left, Kay closed the door. "Do you think Sandy will really come here?" she asked, concern reflected in her soft eyes.

"I don't think so, unless she changes her mind about running away and decides to go back to her mother. She knows we would make her stay here and that we'd call her home or the authorities right away."

Kay's uneasiness kindled. "I suppose you're right, but I can't help wishing that she would. The poor girl is so terribly upset right now. She's got to have help!"

Danny had planned to go out looking for Mr. Cole and possibly for Sandy, but now that he knew the police were covering the area, he changed his mind. Instead, he and Kay went into his study to pray. They asked God to take care of the bewildered, frightened girl wherever she was and to keep her from harm until she was found and brought back home. They were still on their knees when there was a loud, imperative knock on the door.

"I'll answer it." Danny said.

Kay bowed her head and prayed silently. *Dear God, let it be Sandy.*

CHAPTER 10

A SURPRISE VISITOR

Before Danny got to the door, the knock came again. It was a member of the Cole family, but not Sandy. When Danny opened the front door, Mr. Cole was standing there, bloodshot eyes narrowing angrily. "Hello, Mr. Cole, won't you come in?"

Their visitor did not move. "Where's Sandy?" he demanded.

"She's not here."

The distraught father refused to believe him. "Come off it, Orlis! Where is she? What'd you do with her?"

The stench of cheap liquor permeated his clothing and seemed to ooze from every pore.

"My former wife put you up to it, didn't she?" His thick tongue slurred the words.

"I don't have the slightest idea what you're talking about." Danny's tones were icy and impersonal. "But I can tell you this much, my friend, if you are going to stay here and expect Kay and me to talk to you, you're going to be civil to us."

Mr. Cole's manner changed. "Where is she? What's her mother done with her?" He clutched at the door frame to support himself; apparently overcome with desperation, he almost collapsed in his weakened condition.

"Your wife hasn't done anything to Sandy. As near as I can understand from talking to both your wife and the sheriff, Sandy simply ran away on her own."

"I don't believe it!" He spat out the words. "She's not that kind of a girl! Her mother had to do something to her or she'd never have run away!"

"You blame your wife for what's happened to Sandy, and she blames you." Danny Orlis spoke evenly. "I have a hunch that you're both right. Your drinking and your wife's divorce action have caused the trouble."

Mr. Cole ignored Danny's remarks about himself as though they had never been voiced.

"I know she blames me for everything. That's what the sheriff said when he came to talk to me. If I couldn't have proved where I'd been all evening, I'd probably be in jail right now."

Danny surveyed him critically, trying to decide whether it would be wise to try and help. There was little chance of talking to him in the condition he was in at the moment. He would have to sober up first.

"Why don't you come into the kitchen, Mr. Cole," he said, "and we'll have some coffee."

The other man stiffened. "I suppose you think I'm drunk."

"Frankly, you're in a terrible condition, Mr. Cole. You should be sober tonight, of all nights, while they're looking for Sandy."

"I may have had a drink or two, but I'm not drunk. I'll have you know that."

Danny did not argue with him.

"Come on into the kitchen and sit down." Kay took charge of the situation competently. "It will only take a few minutes to make some coffee."

Mr. Cole and Danny sat down at the table across from each other.

"I'll have you know that I'm not drunk. I'm not drunk!" He tried to pound the table with his fist, but it was a pathetic gesture.

It wasn't long until Kay had some black coffee and toast for him. He sipped the coffee as though the very act was painful and protested that he didn't want to eat anything.

"My stomach is so upset I just can't."

"You'd better eat something," Kay told him. "It will help you to get back on your feet."

Mr. Cole eyed her quizzically. "Where do you think Sandy's gone? What's happened to her?"

Kay's frown deepened. "I wish I knew, Mr. Cole. I really wish I knew."

Tears filled his eyes. "If anything happens to her, I'll never forgive myself!"

He drank several cups of black coffee and ate a slice of toast while Danny and Kay sat with him, talking when he wanted to talk and remaining silent when he preferred to say nothing. Gradually his voice became coherent, and a semblance of his quiet dignity came back to his manner. Danny saw that he was a gentleman when he was completely sober, a most likable gentleman. It was hard to believe that alcohol could make such a change in him.

They talked about Sandy for a time and then, inevitably, the subject switched to his drinking habits.

"I don't know what's the matter with me. I used to be able to take a couple of drinks and quit. But now, give me a taste of liquor and I'm gone! I've got to drink everything in sight."

"Would you like to quit?"

Mr. Cole's gaze narrowed. *"Like to quit?"* His harsh voice echoed throughout the room. "I'd give anything I own to quit drinking. You don't know what it's like to have that monkey on your back. Every waking hour I have to fight the urge to drink! I have to force myself to ignore every tavern and every beer or whiskey ad along the highway. I have to battle against the TV commercials and those programs with all their drinking and liquor." He paused, as though recounting those things was enough to begin the battle once more. "And the worst of it is that I'll *never* be free from it!"

Danny's gaze met his, calmly. "You can be."

Mr. Cole eyed him skeptically, as though he was naive and immature.

"You can talk. You don't know what it's like to crave a drink so much that you'd almost give your life for it."

"I've never experienced it, Mr. Cole," Danny went on, shaking his head a few times. "That's true. But I do know how you can be free of the hold that liquor has on you. I can introduce you to the One who can take away your desire to drink."

The other man leaned forward, as if grasping for the life preserver Danny seemed to be throwing to him. "I'd do *anything* to be able to quit *drinking!* Anything!"

"Do you honestly mean that?"

"Just try me and see."

Danny thought of getting his Bible, but he did not immediately. It would be better to talk to Mr. Cole first.

"The Bible tells us that we can do anything in Christ's name, who gives us strength. He can keep you from drinking."

Mr. Cole's anger flared. "I might have known it would have something to do with that childish religion of yours."

"This doesn't have anything to do with religion,"

Danny told him. "I'm talking about the person of the Lord Jesus Christ. He is the One who not only can keep you from drinking, but He can take away the very desire to drink."

Mr. Cole listened curiously. "I've never heard anything like that before. You aren't kidding me, are you?"

"I wouldn't kid you about anything as serious as this. It works. I've seen other men who were hopeless, helpless alcoholics until the Lord Jesus Christ got hold of their lives. I've seen those same men get victory over liquor to the place where they never have to fight alcohol to keep from drinking. They've been delivered from its power."

Danny went on to explain the way of salvation. Mr. Cole professed to have attended church with some degree of regularity until about five years ago when he got mad at the minister and a couple of board members and quit.

With all of his church attendance and the many sermons he had heard, however, Mr. Cole had never been told that he needed Jesus Christ as his Savior. He had never thought of Christ as a person he could know and put his trust in for eternal life. Jesus had been the "example" to him, the "great teacher," the "model for a good life," but that was all. This new concept of Christ was not easy for him to grasp.

Danny continued, however, painstakingly quoting Bible verses that showed that every man was a sinner and worthy of death and that Christ was God's way of reconciling sinful man to Himself.

Mr. Cole listened, eyes widening.

"And this is for me?" He was still uncertain. "You mean that God would accept *me* if I come to Him, after all the wicked things I've done?"

Danny answered him quietly. "Christ told the thief on the cross that he would be with Him in paradise that day, solely because of his faith. And the apostle Paul had actually murdered Christians before he trusted Christ as his Savior." Danny's smile was inviting. "So, why don't you try Him and see?"

Mr. Cole had a few more questions, but it wasn't long before he knelt in the kitchen beside his chair and gave his heart and life to Christ.

After Danny showed him from Scripture that he could know for sure that he was truly a child of God, he left to look for Sandy once more.

"I've got to find her. I've got to tell her what's happened to me!"

"We'll be praying for you." Danny and Kay followed him to the front door. "We'll be praying for all three of you."

"Thanks. We're sure going to need it." He shook hands with both of them once more, impulsively. "I'll be in touch with you, Orlis."

"Fine."

The car was just leaving the drive when the phone rang. It was Sheriff Riley calling for Danny. "I hate to bother you so late at night, but we just had another report that the Cole girl is in your area. I'm going to send some men out to look for her just as soon as I can get them together."

"Is there anything I can do?"

"As a matter of fact, there is. I'd like to have you go outside and look around. There's a possibility that she might have come into the yard but was afraid to go to the house. In that case she just might be in your car or one of the other buildings."

When Danny finished talking on the phone, Del and Doug were standing in the doorway of their bedroom, eyeing Danny and Kay.

"What's all the excitement about?" Doug wanted to know. "What's going on?"

"You'd better go back to bed. It's awfully late."

Del went over to where Danny and Kay were standing. "Who called just now?" he asked.

They glanced quickly at each other as though to ask whether they should tell the boys about Sandy's disappearance.

"I guess there's no need in keeping it from you," Danny said. "Sandy Cole ran away from home tonight."

The boys gasped. "Oh, no!" Doug exclaimed. "Has anyone found out where she's gone?"

Kay shook her head.

"Not yet. But that call was from the sheriff. He wanted Danny to go out and look around the buildings. A report came in that she was headed in this direction."

Both boys had the same idea at once. "Can we go out and look for her too, Danny?"

"Can we?"

He hesitated. He was about to turn them down because it was so late, but he changed his mind. This was an emergency, and it would be good to have a little more help. The sooner they found out if she was nearby, the better it would be for everyone.

"Go get dressed but be quiet so you don't waken DeeDee. There's no use getting her upset tonight if we can help it."

The boys rushed back to the bedroom, dressed with frantic haste, pulling their jeans and sweatshirts on over their pajamas, and returned to the living room.

Danny handed each of them a flashlight.

"Now, we've got to work fast," he said guardedly. "We want to have all the buildings and the area around them covered by the time the sheriff and his men get here. Okay?"

They nodded to show they understood what he wanted them to do.

"I'll take the barn. You guys can start with the smaller buildings."

They went to the granary first, but there was no sign that she had been there. It was the same with the rest of the buildings. A few minutes later they met Danny near the back gate.

"Find anything?" Doug asked.

He shook his head. "How about you?"

"She isn't anywhere close. I can tell you that much. If she was, we'd have found some sort of sign."

"Maybe the sheriff got a bum steer when someone called in that she'd been seen near our place," Danny said.

The boys waited uneasily. Finally, Del spoke up. "What're we going to do now?"

Danny started for the house. "I'd like to look around some more, but I'd better go in. The sheriff ought to be here any minute."

"We could look some more, couldn't we, Del?" Doug said.

"Sure thing."

Danny agreed reluctantly. "Don't be gone too long. We don't want you to get lost, so we have to go out and search for you, too."

"Get lost in these woods!" Del exclaimed. "That'd be the day!"

"Just the same, take it easy. Most anything can happen in the woods after dark."

The boys told him they would go down to the lake and back into the woods a short distance on the assumption that she had gone in that direction.

"Fine, but be as quiet as you can. If she doesn't want to be found, she might hide if she hears you before you get close to her."

The boys left the farmhouse quietly, making their

way down to the lakeshore. Doug wasn't sure they had made a wise move and protested to his brother.

"What would she want in a place like this, anyway? She'd have a terrible time stumbling through the woods in the dark. And, besides, she'd be scared to death being out here alone."

Del shrugged. "Maybe you're right, but I figured if I was running away, the lake is the first place I'd head for. If she was out on the highway someone would be sure to see her."

They whispered as they moved, making their way down to the lake and turning on the narrow, twisting path that paralleled the shore. They paused every few feet to examine the path and the bushes lining it. The flashlight revealed nothing.

"She'd have broken a branch or done something to show that she'd gone this way. She isn't good enough to walk through the bush without leaving some sort of a trail," said Doug.

Del was still determined that they were right. "Maybe so, but there've been so many people using the path lately that we'd have a hard time telling whether Sandy had been along here or not."

At that instant there was a muffled sound on the trail ahead. Del stopped suddenly and grasped his brother by the arm.

"What is it?"

Del put a hand to his lips. "Shh! Somebody's coming!"

CHAPTER 11

TOGETHER AT LAST, PERHAPS

Doug Davis switched off the flashlight he was carrying and pressed into the brush along the narrow path. Del crouched breathlessly behind him. At first the boys thought it must be Sandy, but it couldn't be her, they reasoned. She would have been moving as quietly as possible to avoid being heard.

The boys waited in the gray half-light of night, their lithe bodies becoming tense under the pressure of the moment. In another instant a huge, dark shape lumbered into view.

"Barney!" The word exploded from Del's lips.

The unexpected sound startled the old Indian. He jumped backward half a step, brown eyes focusing intently on the two boys.

"Barney! What're you doing here?"

The Indian was still staring at them, still unable

to believe that they could be out on the trail at such an hour.

"What're you two doing here?" he demanded.

"We came to look for Sandy." Del went on to tell their Indian friend that the girl had run away from home and the police were looking for her. "Danny said they haven't been able to find any trace of her, except for a report that she was seen heading toward our farm. The sheriff called a little while ago and asked Danny to look around, so that's what we did."

Barney chuckled, but there was no real laughter in his voice. "It is the girl who brings me to your house tonight." He was speaking softly as though afraid of being overheard.

"You mean you've seen her? You know where she is?"

Barney reverted to Cree the way he often did when he was disturbed, but after a few words, he caught himself and switched to English.

"Yes, I have seen her. And I know where she is. At this moment she sleeps in my cabin!"

"You're kidding!"

Barney shook his head. "It is the truth," he said simply.

He went on to tell how the girl had stumbled up to his door only a few hours before, frightened and crying. He got up, dressed, and let her in.

"I have never seen anyone so afraid," he went on. "She was afraid of the strange noises she heard in the bush. She was afraid of the darkness and afraid of getting caught and having to return home to live with her mother. She was afraid she would never get to see her dad again and that they would put him in jail."

He paused for breath. "I knew everybody would be worried about her, but she was so upset that I didn't dare leave her until she went to sleep. I was afraid she would guess where I went and run away again. So I fixed some tea and sandwiches and sat and talked with her until she got sleepy. Then I had her go into my bedroom to sleep, and I lay down on the floor and pretended to go to sleep myself." His eyes twinkled. "But I only laid there for a little while until she was asleep. Then I leave to tell Danny."

He hesitated momentarily.

"Why don't you go back and tell him where she is? I'll go back to my cabin and stay in case she wakes up."

"Good idea," Del answered.

"Thanks, Barney. We'll see you in a little while."

The boys scurried back to the house, arriving just as Danny and the sheriff were ready to leave.

"We've found her!" Doug cried. "We've found her!"

The men came running to meet them. "Where is she?" Danny asked. "Is she all right?"

Breathlessly they told Danny and the sheriff about meeting Barney on the trail and how he had gone back to the cabin to stay with her.

"That's fine," Sheriff Riley said. He turned to Danny. "You know this girl, don't you?"

"She's stayed in our home for several weeks."

"I think it would be better if you would go down to the cabin and get her. She wouldn't be nearly as frightened as she would be if I went."

Danny agreed with him. He could only guess how frightened Sandy would be when he went to bring her back. She was terribly upset over the divorce. If she hadn't been, she would never have run away.

Doug and Del pleaded to go with him, but Danny refused.

"You guys had better go home and turn in. You need your sleep."

They protested, but he did not change his mind. Leaving them, he hurried toward Barney's cabin alone. Sandy was still sleeping when he got there, but as soon as she heard voices she got up and came out, keeping her gaze averted so he wouldn't see her tear-reddened eyes.

"Hello, Sandy."

She did not answer his greeting.

"I had a visitor last night."

"Who was it?" she asked angrily. "Mother?"

"No, it was your father. He's been terribly worried about you."

At the mention of her father, Sandy Cole gasped.

"W-w-was he all right? They haven't put him in jail, have they?"

"Why would they do that?"

Hesitantly she blurted out the story of the house

and how her mother threatened to have her father put in jail.

Suddenly he began to understand. "Is this the reason you ran away?"

Sandy did not answer his question with a simple yes or no. "I couldn't stay there and see him go to jail." Anguish darkened her eyes. "I couldn't have Mom come home bragging about what she had done to him."

Danny sat down across from her.

"I'm not an attorney, Sandy, and I don't know much about the law," he said, "but I'm sure your mother can't send your dad to jail for not keeping up the house payments. The only payments the court would send him to jail for not making are those the judge sets."

Her fists clenched and relaxed nervously. "Oh, I hope you're right."

"Why don't we go back to the house, and I'll call the county attorney and find out what he has to say about it."

She paused uneasily. "I'd like to find out for sure, but–"

"Is there some reason you don't want to go back to our place?"

Her gaze met his. "Is Mom there?"

"She wasn't when I left."

"Then I'll go."

When they got back to the Orlis house, Kay had already phoned Mrs. Cole to give her the good news.

"Is she coming here tonight?" Sandy's voice revealed her fears.

"I told her I'd call her when I thought she should come."

"I know what she'll say when she does come. She'll tell me how terrible I am and that I never think of her and the awful things she's had to go through."

Danny stopped her. "Now wait a minute, Sandy. You've got to be reasonable with her as you want her to be with you. This has been a terrible ordeal for both your parents."

Sandy straightened, disbelief clouding her eyes.

"I do understand, Sandy. I know this is hard for you. But I know, too, that the Bible tells us to honor our parents. I'm afraid there isn't much honor for your mother in your attitude right now."

"But you *know* what she's done!"

"I know she's your mother."

Sandy settled back in the chair, folded her arms, slouched, and glared. She had thought he understood. He tried to make her believe that he did. But now he was turning on her and taking her mother's side.

She was surprised when at nine o'clock the next morning he called the county attorney. It was several minutes before he came back to the room where she was sitting.

"Well, I have some good news for you, Sandy,"

he said. "The attorney says that the judge did not stipulate that your dad had to make the house payments. That was his own idea. So there is nothing for you to worry about."

She sat upright. Tears flooded her eyes and trickled down her cheeks. Her dad wouldn't have to go to jail after all!

* * *

Shortly before noon Mrs. Cole came out to get Sandy. She was not crying, but the heavy makeup around her eyes spoke eloquently of the repair work she had had to do to mask the effects of a sleepless night. She came into the Orlis home soberly, scarcely speaking to Danny and Kay.

For the space of half a minute, Sandy and her mother stared at each other without speaking. Then a feeble smile appeared briefly on Mrs. Cole's lips.

"Hello, Sandy," she said. "I'm so thankful that you're all right."

"I–" She tried to speak, but her voice cracked, and she had to stop.

"You'll never know how worried I was. I imagined that all sorts of things had happened to you."

"You shouldn't have been so upset. I can take care of myself."

"You're going home with me, aren't you?"

"I–I guess so–if I can come out here and visit whenever I want to."

"Of course, you can. I'll be happy to let you come any time." The honey almost dripped from Mrs. Cole's voice.

Sandy started out with her mother, but when they were almost to the car, she excused herself and ran back to whisper to Danny. "I almost forgot. Will you find Daddy for me and–and tell him that I'm all right?"

"I'll go right out and look for him."

As soon as Mrs. Cole's car was out of sight, Danny and Kay went to theirs and began cruising around Fairview. Neither of them wanted to admit it, but the bars had most of their attention. Finally, Kay spotted him in a park, talking to a man who looked as unfortunate as Mr. Cole did. But now his face was clean, and he had shaved. They swung over to the curb, and Mr. Cole hurried toward the car. When he saw their smiles, he said, "You've found my daughter."

Mr. Cole was glad that Sandy had been found unharmed. He wanted to talk with her, but her mother had already taken her back to town. Kay read the disappointment in his eyes.

"Why don't you stop by the house and see her?"

He didn't think that was possible, but it was worth a try, he acknowledged. All the way to town he prayed for his former wife, asking God to help her understand what he was trying to say. When he first drove up, he was afraid she wasn't home, but as he nosed into the driveway, he saw the back of her car extending beyond the house. For some reason she had pulled close to the kitchen door, almost hiding the car from the street.

"What do you want?" she demanded belligerently when she saw him at the door.

"I'd like to talk to you," he said politely. She stepped back, her hand on the doorknob. "Please, it'll only take a few minutes."

"All right, but only on the condition that you'll leave whenever I ask you to."

Once inside and seated, he cleared his throat and began hesitantly. "I came to the end of myself last night. I turned my life over to God."

Her eyes widened and her mouth fell open. She made no attempt to hide her surprise. "You've got to be kidding!"

"I'm telling you the truth. I finally saw that I wasn't getting anywhere trying to fight the bottle myself. So I confessed my sin and turned my life over to Jesus Christ. I'm a Christian now and I–"

"*You?*" She threw back her head and laughed.

He stared at her in disbelief and tried to explain once more, but her laughter came again, harsh and scornful.

"Just wait until our friends hear that!"

In spite of her disdain, he continued doggedly,

asking her forgiveness for the terrible way he had treated her.

Bitterness twisted her lips. "Why should I? I want to see you suffer the way you've made me suffer."

Mr. Cole was surprised at the lack of anger in his voice. Indeed, he felt no anger for her, only compassion and genuine sorrow for the things he had done during the last few months of their marriage.

"I don't blame you for feeling the way you do."

She got a cigarette from the pack on the mantel and lit it deliberately, blowing a thin stream of smoke in his direction.

"You can quit faking it now. Your little scheme isn't going to work."

Her mirth echoed in his ears as he left the house and made his way slowly to his car. He should have known that she wouldn't understand, but he was glad he had gone and talked to her. Slowly he drove down the street.

* * *

Sandy hadn't thought much about going to church the next morning. She and her mother hadn't been going lately. But she decided she wanted to go this time. She was surprised at the fact that she enjoyed going to church a great deal. The service was almost over when she glanced at the section to her right.

She gasped aloud. There was her dad! And in church! She could scarcely believe it!

As soon as the service was over, she ran to him and threw herself into his arms. "Oh, Daddy!" Her voice broke.

He held her tenderly, repeating her name over and over again. It was some time before Sandy was able to control herself enough to speak.

"I–I was afraid that I'd never see you again!" he whispered. He patted the back of her head awkwardly.

"I could hardly believe it was you when I saw you a few minutes ago," she answered.

He laughed self-consciously. "I can't say that I blame you, but I guess I do owe you an explanation." He was fumbling for words. "Something happened to me, Sandy. The night you ran away, I–I came face to face with myself for the first time. I saw what I was doing to you and–and to your mother. I met the person of the Lord Jesus Christ. I confessed my sin and asked Him to save me and clean up this miserable life of mine."

This couldn't be for real! Sandy told herself. *Not my dad!*

"I–I'm sorry for all the heartache and sadness I've caused you and your mother, Sandy. Will you forgive me?"

Tears flooded her eyes and ran unheeded down her cheeks. This wasn't the way he was before. She could scarcely believe it was him.

"Of course." She wiped her eyes.

Joy flooded over the bewildered girl. Her mother would soon know if she didn't already. She would see the change that had come about in his life, and it might be that she would take him back and their family would be together once more.

But, even as she considered that, she realized that a lot of things had to happen before the divorce could be erased. That didn't keep her from being excited and happy, however. She didn't understand a lot about being a Christian, but she knew her dad was sincere in what he said. This time she was sure that the drinking would stop. He had God to help him. She even tried to pray silently, thanking God for what had happened and asking Him to give her dad the strength and courage he needed to stay sober and live the kind of life he ought to live.

She had never been so happy in all her life.